She let Felipe draw her into his arms

His lips on hers were like a caress to start with, but gradually he began to exert more pressure, and she felt her knees trembling. She shifted position slightly, not realizing what it would do to him. He groaned and forced her mouth open with an urgency she did not understand. No one had ever kissed her like that.

She found her hands had tangled in the hair at the nape of his neck. Felipe's hands molded her closer. He began to tremble, and Stacy, not aware of his struggle, held him close. With a stifled groan he pushed her from him.

"I'm sorry, Stacy, I did not mean to...."

"I don't understand," she said plaintively.

He took her in his arms again. "Oh, Stacy, you're such a child! What am I going to do with you?"

WELCOME
TO THE WONDERFUL WORLD
OF *Harlequin Romances*

Interesting, informative and entertaining,
each Harlequin Romance portrays an appealing
and original love story. With a varied array
of settings, we may lure you on an African safari,
to a quaint Welsh village, or an exotic Riviera
location—anywhere and everywhere that adventurous
men and women fall in love.

As publishers of Harlequin Romances, we're
extremely proud of our books. Since 1949,
Harlequin Enterprises has built its publishing
reputation on the solid base of quality and
originality. Our stories are the most popular
paperback romances sold in North America; every
month, six new titles are released and sold at
nearly every book-selling store in Canada and the
United States.

A free catalog listing all Harlequin Romances
can be yours by writing to the

HARLEQUIN READER SERVICE,
(In the U.S.) 1440 South Priest Drive, Tempe, AZ 85281
(In Canada) Stratford, Ontario, N5A 6W2

We sincerely hope you enjoy reading
this Harlequin Romance.

Yours truly,

THE PUBLISHERS
Harlequin Romances

To Be or Not to Be

by

SUE BYFIELD

Harlequin Books

TORONTO • NEW YORK • LOS ANGELES • LONDON
AMSTERDAM • PARIS • SYDNEY • HAMBURG
STOCKHOLM • ATHENS • TOKYO • MILAN

Original hardcover edition published in 1982
by Mills & Boon Limited

ISBN 0-373-02529-7

Harlequin Romance first edition February 1983

CHAPTER ONE

STACY peered out of the plane window. Miles below the sea shimmered like deep blue crystal. Excitement welled up inside her; this was her first trip abroad and, as she was on her way to see her sister who had married two years before and moved to Menorca with her Spanish husband, she was doubly excited. Stacy had been planning this trip ever since Christine, her sister, had left home. Unfortunately, exams had prevented an earlier visit, apart from the fact that her father could have ill afforded the fare.

Stacy's stomach lurched as the plane took a steep dive towards the tiny airport of Mahón. To take her mind off the landing she took out her compact and surveyed her face critically. Deep blue eyes stared back at her, wide and excited. She applied fresh lipstick, ran a brush through her long fair hair and prepared herself for the imminent descent.

Thirty minutes later, she was standing in the spacious airport baggage collection point watching the luggage travel slowly around on a conveyor belt. After spotting her cases she heaved them off the runner and made for the exit. She waved away the porters who besieged her from all sides, trying to take the cases from her, and did not notice the appreciative gazes of the airport guards, their dark eyes following her progress with interest. Indeed she made an interesting picture in her denim dungarees and white blouse, her slender figure struggling with two heavy cases and her long hair flying. Just as she reached the doors she spotted the bright auburn hair which could only belong to her sister and hurried out towards her.

'Chrissy, Chrissy—I'm here!' she called excitedly.

The auburn head turned sharply and the face lit up. Stacy dropped her cases and hurled herself at her sister with gusto.

'Oh, Chris, it's so good to see you!' she cried as the older girl picked her up and swung her around. 'You look great—so brown. Life is certainly treating you well, by the look of it!'

'It's good to see you too, darling,' her sister replied. 'I hardly recognised you, you've grown up so much.' She wiped tears furiously from her eyes.

Stacy laughed. 'Of course I've grown up, I'm eighteen now!'

'My, my,' her sister replied sombrely, 'you're almost an old woman.'

Stacy grinned and looked about her in wonder. Heat bore down on her head like a heavy weight; she had not expected it to be so hot.

'Well,' said Chris, picking up one of Stacy's cases, 'we'd better get going. It will take about half an hour or so to get to Cala Galdaña, then you can have a quick wash before we have lunch. I want to hear about everyone and everything. The car's this way—come on.' She headed off towards a bright red Seat and opened the door. Stacy followed. 'How did you like the flight?' Chris asked.

'Well, I survived it,' Stacy replied, 'but it wasn't my favourite experience. The stewardesses were very kind, though, and the food was O.K.'

'Good, I'm glad you liked the food anyway!' Chrissy chided her.

'Wow, it's so hot!' Stacy exclaimed, lifting her hair

from the back of her neck. 'I didn't know anywhere could be as hot as this.'

Chris laughed. 'You've arrived at the hottest time of the day, actually, it'll cool down a bit later. We'll open all the windows and hope the breeze will keep you cool.'

They seated themselves in the car and Stacy looked around appreciatively. 'I like this, Chris,' she said, waving her hand around.

'Yes, Fernando bought it for me. It's just ideal for nipping around in; not too big for me to handle.'

Stacy leaned back in her seat and closed her eyes as her sister drove across the island. She wanted to see everything, but the hot sun hurt her eyes, and she had packed her sunglasses in one of the cases. She thought about her sister's fairy-tale romance with the handsome Spaniard she had met on holiday three years ago. Everyone had thought it was a typical holiday romance that would fizzle out as soon as the holiday was over—but it hadn't. Fernando Moreno had come to visit Christine six weeks later and Christine had been invited over to meet his parents. Then a year later they had been married in a small church in Birmingham. It had been a strange wedding. All Fernando's family had arrived by private charter jet, the older ladies all in black, the younger ones in obviously expensive modern clothing. The old men had been gnarled and brown, like walnuts, the younger ones flirtatious. Things had been complicated by the language barrier, although most of the younger people had spoken English very well.

'Hey, you haven't heard a word I've been saying to you!' her sister's voice cut through Stacy's thoughts.

She turned quickly to her sister and smiled, 'Sorry, Chris, I was daydreaming. What did you say?'

Chris shook her head 'It doesn't matter. We'll be there soon; look over there, you get a fabulous view of the bay as we turn the corner.'

They turned off the almost straight main road and headed up a winding hilly one to the left. Stacy caught a glimpse of high cliffs topped with trees, blue sparkling sea and a few yachts dotted about it. It was a breathtaking sight and it was gone before she had time to absorb it properly.

'Oh, couldn't we stop and have a longer look?' she begged.

Chris shook her head. 'You'll get a better view still from the villa, and I'm hungry, even if you're not,' she finished with a cheeky grin.

The car stopped outside the gates of a large villa with a tree-lined drive leading to the front door. Chris went to open the gates and Stacy sat spellbound in the car, taking in all the affluence around her. Chris climbed back into the driver's seat and drove through the gates.

'You never told me he was a millionaire!' Stacy accused her sister.

Chris laughed as she stopped the car outside the front steps of the villa. 'Fernando isn't a millionaire; he's quite well off, but not *that* well off!'

'But this is fabulous! When you sent us the photos we didn't realise it was so—so—well, you know.'

Her sister smiled. 'I'm glad you like it. Now you can understand why I don't miss England all that much, except for you and Daddy. All I have here compensates for what I've left behind.'

Stacy opened the door and stepped out into the tremendous heat of the early afternoon. After smoothing down her dungarees, which had started to cling to her, she helped her sister remove some bags from the car, but when she reached for the cases Chris held up her hand. 'Leave those, Stacy, Paco will collect them; he's our handyman—husband of Mrs Sanchez who I'm taking you to meet now.'

She began to walk towards the door, leaving Stacy staring after her in surprise. Fancy being able to afford a handyman! She followed her sister through the door and into the cool, dark interior. The hallway was large and a smell of polish hung in the air. A winding wrought-iron staircase went off to the left and a polished table stood opposite holding an enormous bowl of flowers.

'Come on, Stacy—you're in a dream,' Chris chided. She led the way into a large kitchen, equipped with all modern conveniences. 'I want you to meet Chezzie before you go up to have a wash,' she told her, 'she's been dying to meet you. She's a sort of housekeeper.'

A large rotund lady detached herself from the cupboard she had been searching in and walked across the room to them. She was completely dressed in black and her hair, also dark but with a liberal scattering of grey threads, was scraped up into a tidy bun. She had a merry face and infectious smile which detracted from the severity of her dress.

'Chezzie, this is my little sister Stacy,' Chris announced. She turned to Stacy. 'We call her Chezzie because I can't pronounce her first name properly.'

The older woman grasped Stacy's hands and beamed at her. 'I welcome you, *señorita*. You are very pretty, just like your sister. What beautiful hair, it is like the corn with the sun shining on it.'

'Oh,' Stacy exclaimed, unused to such compliments, 'th—thank you. I'm very pleased to meet you.'

Chris explained, 'Chezzie is an angel, she's been a real help to me since I've been here, helping me to settle down and teaching me the customs. I don't know what we'd do without her.'

They chatted amiably for a few minutes and then Chris led Stacy away. 'Come on, I'll show you your room and you can have a quick wash before lunch.'

Stacy followed her, still in a dream. The winding staircase led to a thickly carpeted corridor, with doors leading off on either side.

'This is your room, I hope you'll like it,' said Chris, opening a door on the left.

The room was beautiful, bathed in sunlight and decorated in typical Spanish style. As a contrast to the white walls and ceiling, the curtains were pink velvet and the bedspread matched. There was a fluffy pink rug on the polished floor.

'It's absolutely lovely, I've never seen such a beautiful room,' Stacy enthused. 'It makes my room at home look a bit sick, doesn't it?'

Chris hugged her younger sister affectionately. 'I was a bit overpowered at first, but you get used to it in time. I don't mean I take it for granted or anything, but it becomes more normal, if you see what I mean. I couldn't write about it all in letters, I wanted you to see for yourself. And I'm really glad you have,' she finished, hugging Stacy to her once more before walking farther into the room.

After she had showed Stacy around, Chris left her to freshen up. Stacy sat on the bed and looked about her. 'Fancy Chris having all this,' she mused. She did not feel in the least bit jealous, only surprised. She thought of her meagre wardrobe, packed away tidily in the suitcases. It wasn't really fit for these sort of surroundings, but studying had taken up all the money her father could afford, there had been no room for luxuries. Stacy roused herself and walked over to the bathroom, through a pair of louvred doors. The bathroom suite was also pink and a full mirror covered the wall over the bath. She decided to take a quick shower and wash her hair, which felt grubby after her long journey. She returned to the bedroom ten minutes later, her hair wrapped turban-fashion in a white towel. She selected an uncreased pink summer dress from her suitcase and found a pair of matching sandals. After combing her wet hair into a ponytail she went in search of her sister, and lunch.

She found Chris in a large lounge off the hallway. She looked up as Stacy approached. 'Ah, there you are. You look great; I can see my little sister is going to steal a few hearts while she's here.'

Stacy pulled a face at her.

'Come and sit down and let's eat—I'm starving,' said Chris.

'Dear old Chris,' Stacy replied, 'still eating like a horse and never putting on an ounce.'

Her sister surveyed her critically. 'You don't carry any spare weight around yourself, do you? Have you been starving yourself, or going on one of these silly diets?' she asked.

'No,' Stacy shook her head, 'it's just the way I'm made.'

'I'm sure you look thinner than when I last saw you,' Chris answered, unconvinced.

'Puppy fat,' replied Stacy, sitting down.

The room was large and airy and french windows across one wall led out on to a patio with white

wrought-iron furniture and a profusion of gaily
coloured flowers bordering a lawn.

'We'll stay in here for now,' said Chris, seeing
Stacy's longing look at the garden. 'I don't want
you to get sunstroke on your first day here.'

An hour later, after drinking coffee and talking
non-stop about old times and the latest news from
England, Chris advised Stacy to have a siesta. 'We
keep late hours here, dinner isn't until nine and if
you don't have a rest you'll probably fall asleep in
your pudding!' she quipped. 'It takes a lot out of
you, travelling.'

Stacy agreed and went to lie down for a while,
not expecting to be able to sleep. She awoke some
time later and couldn't remember where she was.
She raised herself on one elbow and, pushing her
hair out of her eyes, gazed about. Memory flooded
back and she lay down again, closing her eyes. She
must have slept again, for she awoke with a start as
a car door slammed outside. She hastily looked at
her watch. It was seven-thirty! She couldn't believe
it! Hurriedly she brushed her hair and washed her
face and, after straightening out her dress, made her
way back downstairs. As she approached the lounge
door she heard voices, that of her sister and a much
deeper one which she presumed was Fernando.
Stacy entered the room and realised she had been
mistaken. The man talking to Chris was certainly
not Fernando. Although similar in appearance, he
was taller, darker skinned and quite attractive. He
rose as she approached and towered over her, smiling. Chris stood too and introduced the tall stranger.

'Stacy, this is Felipe Cuevas, our next door neighbour and good friend. Felipe, this is my little sister
Stacy.'

He held out his hand and Stacy raised hers to it. An electric shock shot along her arm at the cool hard pressure he exerted.

'How do you do,' she said in a quiet voice.

'I am very pleased to see you again,' Felipe told her in a deep voice. His eyes, which were almost black, appraised her and she felt herself turning pink. He released her hand and she sat down on the couch next to her sister, her knees feeling incapable of supporting her any longer. She wondered what he meant by saying he was pleased to see her again; she was sure she would have remembered meeting him before.

'Felipe is coming to dinner tonight,' Chris informed her. 'We thought it would be a sort of welcome party for you.'

'Lovely,' Stacy replied.

'Do you feel better after your rest?' her sister enquired.

'Oh yes, I do. I didn't realise I was so tired. I must have fallen straight to sleep.'

Felipe Cuevas shifted his position and looked at her. 'I do not suppose you remember me Stacy, but I was at your sister's wedding.'

She registered his deep voice, pleasantly accented, and tried desperately to remember him.

'I'm afraid I don't remember—everything was a bit hectic that day. I'm sorry . . .'

He shrugged his broad shoulders. 'Of course you wouldn't. But you were a bridesmaid, so I remember you. I must say you looked delightful in your long dress.'

Stacy felt herself blushing again and was annoyed to think that this man could embarrass her so easily. She managed a brief smile at him and turned to

Chris in an effort to regain composure.

'What time will Fernando be home? I can't wait to see him again.'

'Oh, in about half an hour I should say,' Chris told her, 'he's been over to Majorca today on business. I expect he'll be all in.'

'Oh well,' Stacy grasped at an opportunity to delay dinner with Felipe Cuevas, 'we could put our dinner party off if you like, I shouldn't want him to put himself out for me.'

'Rubbish,' replied her sister. 'He'll be perfectly all right after a shower and a glass of sherry. He's been looking forward to you coming. We haven't had any of my family to stay since we were married. And it hasn't been possible to get over to England. We can't let an occasion like this slip by unnoticed.' She rose and walked over to the cocktail cabinet. 'What would you like, Stacy?'

'I'll have a Cinzano and lemonade, please.'

Soon after Felipe Cuevas excused himself and departed to get ready for dinner. Stacy returned to her room and set out her clothes, deciding what to wear. She chose a long halter-necked dress in a pale shade of green crêpe which she knew suited her and laid it out on the bed while she applied a touch of make-up. Half an hour later she again descended the stairs and headed for the lounge. Chris was already there and so was her husband, Fernando. He came towards Stacy, tall and dark, as she remembered him, his even teeth showing up white against his dark complexion.

'Stacy—my, my, you have grown up so since I last saw you!' He embraced her and held her away from him to look at her face. He turned to his wife and in a teasing voice said, 'I do believe she is nearly as beautiful as you, Christine. Apart from the hair colour you are like twins.'

Chris aimed a mock punch at her husband and he caught her hand and held it. 'Come off it, Fernando,' she replied. 'Stacy's a knock-out, I could see Felipe eyeing her up this afternoon when he came round.'

'Knock-out?' Fernando queried. 'What is this "knock-out"? It does not sound at all pleasant!'

Chris and Stacy laughed. At that moment there was a knock on the lounge door and Felipe Cuevas walked in, tall and slender in a cream lounge suit and black shirt. He obviously had a good tailor, thought Stacy, his suit fitted like a glove.

'I hope I am not disturbing anything,' he said, with the air of someone who knew he wasn't.

Fernando released the girls and went to shake Felipe by the hand. 'Not at all. We were just discussing the merits of Stacy here and we came to the conclusion that she has grown into a beautiful young lady.'

'Oh, please,' Stacy begged, very embarrassed at the turn of the conversation, 'can't we talk about something else?'

'Now, now, Fernando,' his wife chided, 'Stacy isn't used to you Spaniards yet—let's have a drink and change the subject before she expires with embarrassment!'

'Very well,' said Fernando. 'What will you have Stacy?'

'I—er—I think I'll have a Martini and lemonade, please,' she replied.

'Felipe?—the usual?'

'Please.'

He poured out Stacy's drink and handed it to her,

turning back to the drinks cabinet and pouring Felipe a liberal measure of whisky on the rocks and passing it to him.

'Here is to a happy holiday,' said Felipe, raising his glass to Stacy.

'Thank you,' she said, blushing.

'Yes, happy holiday,' Fernando agreed.

'Have you anything special planned?' Felipe asked.

'Well, not exactly,' Chris replied. 'As you know, Fernando has to work. You're keeping him pretty busy in that company of yours.'

'Well, he is the manager—I do not tell him when to work. It is just unfortunate that he is in the middle of arranging a substantial contract at this moment. I am sure he will be able to take some days off.'

'Oh, of course I shall,' Fernando replied, frowning at his wife.

'Well, if I can be of any help do not hesitate to let me know,' said Felipe.

'I'm sure we'll manage . . .' Chris began.

'That is very good of you,' Fernando interrupted. 'It would be nice to arrange some mutual entertainment. I am sure Stacy would enjoy that.'

'She's hardly had time to settle in yet—give her a chance to get her breath back,' Chris said irritably as the dinner gong sounded.

The dinner was delicious. The oblong dining room was elegantly furnished with a huge mahogany table in the centre and high-backed Spanish style chairs on either side of it. Stacy felt like royalty dining there. The melon starter was very refreshing and the paella which followed was new to her.

'You've got to learn to like paella,' Chris had said. 'We thought it would be a fitting start to your holiday to have it for dinner on your first night. What do you think?'

'It's nice,' Stacy replied. 'The streaky bacon tasted strange, though.'

'Streaky bacon?' Chris queried.

'I think she means the squid,' Fernando told her, trying not to laugh.

'Squid!?' Stacy repeated, an appalled expression on her face. She felt annoyed when they all started to laugh.

'It's not poisonous,' Chris told her. 'If we hadn't told you you wouldn't have bothered about it.'

They had an enormous slice of gâteau each to finish off their meal, and Stacy had to admit to her sister that she couldn't quite finish it.

'It's beautiful, Chris, but I'm so full up I'll burst if I eat any more.'

'Oh don't eat it, then,' her sister replied teasingly, 'we don't want you to make a mess by exploding on our carpet!'

The only disconcerting part of the meal was that she sat opposite Felipe Cuevas and was conscious of her every move as he seemed to be watching her all the time. The conversation, however, had flowed quite easily, and eventually they retired to the *sala* for coffee.

'Did you enjoy your flight?' Fernando asked her. 'I believe you have never flown before.'

'Well,' she replied, 'as I told Chris, I wasn't very happy about it. You go such a long way up! But the stewardesses were very nice. I think it would have been better if I'd had somebody with me—I couldn't hold anybody's hand!'

Felipe Cuevas turned to her. 'It is a pity I was not on the same flight,' he said, a gentle smile playing on his lips. 'I would have been quite happy to hold your hand.'

Stacy blushed scarlet at his words.

'You've made her speechless,' said Chris from across the room. 'She's not used to being chatted up by the likes of you, Felipe.'

'I think she will have many opportunities to remedy that,' Felipe continued, 'I am sure there will be many of my countrymen willing to try.'

'Would you like a glass of sherry or something, Stacy?' Chris asked, changing the subject quickly.

'Oh—er—yes, please. Sweet.'

'One sweet sherry coming up,' Chris repeated.

The day had taken its toll on Stacy and before long she began to feel sleepy. She could have curled up quite happily on one of the comfortable sofas in Chris's lounge. She was suddenly aware of Felipe's dark eyes regarding her.

'I think your little sister is getting sleepy, Chris, it must have been a long eventful day for her,' he said.

'I'm all right—really,' Stacy objected.

Chris agreed, 'Yes, you're looking a bit tired, darling. Have you had enough?'

Stacy shrugged her shoulders. 'I suppose I am a bit tired. I can't think why I should be, though—I slept for most of the afternoon. I hate to think I've wasted any of my holiday sleeping.'

Chris laughed. 'Everybody has to sleep. You'll feel fighting fit in the morning. It takes some time to get adjusted to the heat.'

'Well,' said Stacy, standing up, 'I'll say goodnight, then. It's been a lovely evening. The meal was delicious—except for the squid!' She walked over to where Chris was sitting and kissed her on the cheek. She wasn't sure whether to do the same to Fernando, but decided she would. 'It's been nice meeting you, *señor*,' she said, turning to Felipe Cuevas and wishing she could think of something more inspiring to say.

'Oh, please, call me Felipe,' he begged. 'We do not stand on ceremony here. We are all friends. I expect I shall be seeing a lot more of you anyway—I only live next door. You will find me encroaching on your sister's hospitality quite frequently.'

'Yes,' Chris said jokingly, 'you'd think Felipe didn't have a home to go to, he spends a lot of time round here.'

'That is because he is our friend and knows he is welcome,' Fernando joined in.

'Well, I'll see you in the morning, then,' Stacy said to Chris and Fernando, very conscious of the fact that Felipe Cuevas was still holding her hand.

'Goodnight Stacy,' he said softly, and she attempted a shy smile. '*Hasta mañana*,' he added.

She had no idea what it meant, but she nodded, trying to extricate her hand from his, but he did not let her go.

'You must come over to my villa for dinner one night soon, hm?' he said.

'That would be lovely,' she replied.

'Good, I will arrange it with Chris, then. Goodnight, sleep well.' He lifted Stacy's hand and bent his head to kiss it. She felt the pressure of his lips for a fleeting moment and then he released her.

She walked out of the room as quickly as she could to hide the telltale flush that was about to overtake her. As she went up the stairs to her bedroom she felt the thrill of excitement rush through her again, as she had on the aircraft. 'I'm going to enjoy this holiday,' she said to herself, 'I'm sure I am.'

*

Felipe Cuevas left the Moreno household an hour later and walked slowly back to his own. He stopped by a huge bougainvillea in full bloom to light a cheroot. The face of Stacy came into his mind again. He had had a shock when he had seen her. She had certainly changed—not in looks so much, but in the maturity of them. When he had attended his friend's wedding she had looked like a pretty schoolgirl, but he had remembered her. And now she was a beautiful young woman. He threw away the half-smoked cheroot and ground it out with unnecessary ferocity. She was much too young for him—why, she had only just left school! He made his way into his villa, a puzzled frown marring his features.

The following morning after breakfast Chris had shown Stacy around her home. Stacy was delighted with the swimming pool, which was almost as big as her local baths at home, but the location was definitely an improvement. She and Chris were sitting sipping iced chocolate and talking when Felipe Cuevas appeared through a parting in the bushes surrounding the pool. He was wearing only a pair of navy swimming trunks which accentuated the long, lean length of his body and his dark skin. He had a towel slung around his neck. Stacy immediately felt hot and uncomfortable, and she was mesmerised by the power which his body seemed to emit.

'Good morning, ladies,' he greeted them. 'Not disturbing you, am I?' He sat down on one of the loungers and removed the towel from around his neck.

After they had greeted him Chris explained his presence to Stacy. 'Felipe's pool filter has backed up, so he's using ours for his morning swim until it's mended.'

'What a nuisance,' Stacy mumbled, cursing herself for a fool for being so gauche when he was around.

Chris left them to fetch Felipe a drink and Stacy sat in silence, desperately trying to think of something worthwhile to say.

'Do you think you will enjoy your stay on Menorca?' Felipe asked her.

She jumped, 'Oh, yes—I know I will,' she told him. 'Apart from seeing Chris and Fernando again, this place is beautiful, really beautiful.'

'Good,' he replied, bowing his head in a typically foreign way. 'Do you have a job to go back to when you return to England?'

'No. I wanted to come and see Chris as soon as I'd finished my exams. I'll look for one when I get back. Chris paid for me to come over,' she added. 'Well, I suppose it was Fernando really.'

'So you have no need to rush back to England, then,' Felipe mused.

Stacy shrugged her shoulders and shook her head.

He looked out over the pool. 'Are you going to have a swim?' he asked suddenly.

'Well, I was,' she hedged, not liking the thought of Felipe's dark eyes scrutinising her without her towelling wrap on.

'Come on, then,' he urged. 'We will both have a swim, I shall then enjoy my drink more.'

He stood up and held out his hand. Stacy stood up too and slowly released the belt of her jacket, taking it off and putting it on her chair. Then she took Felipe's outstretched hand and once again felt hers enveloped in a cool steely grip. He led her towards the pool and smiled down at her, his eyes taking in her appearance from head to foot. In her tiny red bikini she felt inadequately dressed in front of him, though she imagined that the sight of a woman's body was nothing new to Felipe Cuevas. She could feel herself beginning to blush again and releasing her hand from his she jumped straight into the water to hide it. The contrast of the cold water against her heated skin made her gasp. She felt Felipe jump in a second later and when she emerged his head popped up beside her. His hair was plastered against his head and his smile seemed even whiter than usual. She struck out across the pool and was surprised to find that he was still beside her.

Chris was now back with Felipe's drink. She shouted across the water, 'You're not trying to outpace Felipe, are you, darling?—you'll never do it. He swims like a fish!'

Felipe laughed. 'Your sister is an excellent swimmer, Chris. We must invite her to spend a day on my boat.' He looked down at Stacy. 'Would you like that?'

'Yes, I would,' she told him, trying not to look away from the dark eyes. She started swimming back towards her sister to escape, but Felipe followed her again and was waiting for her when she reached the other end. As she wiped the hair out of her eyes she suddenly felt two strong hands encircle her waist, and for a second she was held against the hard slippery body behind her. 'Oh!' she yelped as she was deposited in a heap on the rim of the pool.

In one lithe movement Felipe hoisted himself out of the water and held out a hand to help her up. He did not loose it until they were back at the table. Stacy was very confused. She liked Felipe, but she was frightened of the effect he had upon her. Every time he looked at her she could feel something not quite tangible pass between them, and she was too naïve to realise what it was. All her experience—and that wasn't much—had been acquired with boys at school and she was quite unprepared for the overpowering presence of Felipe.

'What are you going to do today?' he asked Chris.

'I don't know yet. We might go to Ciudadela and have a look at the shops or perhaps to one of the beaches, like Son Bou. What would you like to do, Stacy?'

As Stacy opened her mouth to answer, the telephone rang and Chris excused herself to answer it. She returned a few minutes later looking pensive. 'Oh dear, that was Fernando, he's going to bring a business colleague home to lunch. It's a bit unexpected, but there's nothing he can do about it. An important contract—you understand,' she looked at Stacy appealingly.

Before she could say more Felipe joined the conversation. 'I would be quite happy to show Stacy some of the island. I'm free today and I would very much enjoy a drive. It would be nice to act the tourist again.'

Chris's face lit up at the suggestion, but Stacy wasn't so sure.

'I don't mind staying here, really. I could sit around the pool and sunbathe.'

'Oh, Stacy, it's a good idea, Felipe's got a lovely car and he's much better qualified to show you the sights than I am. I should feel better if you'd go with him. I don't like to think of you sitting here on your own while I supervise a business lunch.'

Stacy couldn't refuse.

'O.K.,' she said, 'if you don't mind.' She looked at Felipe.

'Not at all,' he told her, standing up. 'I will go and get ready. Will you be ready in half an hour?'

'Yes, that's plenty of time,' she replied, and he saluted Chris and walked back through the bushes.

'You needn't have said that,' she told her sister. 'I would have been quite happy here.'

Chris looked at her sister in surprise. 'But I thought you'd jump at the chance to go with him. He is rather dishy, let's face it. I know a lot of girls who would envy you, believe me.'

'Yes, but . . . oh, never mind. I suppose I'd better go and get ready,' Stacy replied.

They both went to her bedroom and sorted out a dress and cardigan to wear. Stacy didn't think a cardigan necessary, but Chris explained that Felipe's car had an open top and it might get chilly.

'Pack a swimsuit, darling, you might be in need of a swim later on,' she advised.

Half an hour later Stacy went to meet Felipe in the hall. He had fetched his car and parked outside the front door. She was delighted with the silver-grey Mercedes. He opened the door and handed her in, shutting it behind him. After walking around the bonnet he eased himself in behind the wheel. In close proximity, Stacy was acutely aware of him and tried, without being noticed, to move farther along the seat. The look he gave her told her that he had noticed. She looked away and waved to Chris, who was standing by the door. The powerful engine sprang into life and they were away.

It was exhilarating travelling along with the wind blowing through her hair. It was dry in no time.

'You do not object to having the roof off, do you?'

Felipe asked her. 'I thought it would be more comfortable like this.'

'Not at all, I love it.' Stacy replied.

'Shall we go to Ciudadela first?' he asked.

'If you like—I don't really know where I'm going anyway, so I'll leave it up to you,' she told him.

'Ciudadela it is, then. It used to be the Moorish capital until they transferred it to Mahón. There is a port there and on a clear day you can see Majorca.'

'Lovely,' Stacy replied, disturbed after looking at his strong profile and longing to brush the black hair out of his eyes as it blew across his face with the wind.

'You do not object to coming out with me, I hope?' he asked suddenly, an edge to his voice.

'No, whatever makes you think that? It was very kind of you to offer,' she replied.

'Yes,' he smiled to himself, 'very kind. You do not seem to feel at ease in my company—I wonder why?'

'I . . . I just didn't want to impose on you, that's all,' she told him, not quite knowing what to say.

'I am sure you will not waste my time,' he answered, turning and smiling down into her upturned face. She was acutely conscious of the fact that he was in control and felt a definite urge to get out of the car and run, even though her subconscious urged her to stay. She turned to look out of the side window. The countryside was rather barren, with some olive trees protruding from the middle of rocky fields and the occasional skinny cow sheltering beneath them from the sun. She was surprised to see fields of watermelons growing on the hillsides, seemingly in the middle of nowhere.

Ciudadela was a lovely old town. The Moorish

influence was very much in evidence, with arched
frontages to the buildings, and the main street had a
cloistered walk in front of the shops. There was even
an old windmill in one of the squares, but its sails
were missing. Felipe took Stacy to see the ships
docked in the port and to the Council building from
whose balcony they could watch the world go by.
She found that he was a good guide and began to
enjoy her sightseeing trip—so long as they kept off
personal subjects.

It was very hot and Stacy began to feel the beginnings of a headache. She put her hand on top of
her head, feeling the heat of the sun bearing down
on her, and Felipe noticed the movement.

'You are suffering from the sun, I think.' He smote
his forehead with the palm of his hand. 'I am an
imbecile! I should have warned you to wear a hat.
Come, we must remedy this immediately!' He pulled
her under the Moorish arches of the main shopping
street and into a small shop, dark and cool and out
of the glare of the sun. 'Please choose yourself a hat,
Stacy, we cannot have you getting sunstroke. Your
hair is very fair, you have no protection.' He fingered
a strand of her hair thoughtfully and Stacy hurriedly
walked across to the hat stall.

She looked at the collection before her and
selected a simple straw creation, with ribbons hanging down the back. Walking back to the mirror, she
felt Felipe's eyes following her. It looked good.
Suddenly another pair of eyes were watching her
reflection.

'That looks very attractive, Stacy,' Felipe said
quietly, and she felt herself tremble as his hand closed
around her upper arm to lead her to the cashpoint.
As he attempted to pay for the hat she complained,

'No, please, I can pay for it, I have some money with me.'

'That is quite all right. I will pay,' Felipe answered, and his tone brooked no argument.

He handed it to her and she put it on. 'Thank you—very much,' she mumbled, and turned out of the shop. They walked around a few more alleyways, peering in through the windows of shops as they went. Stacy bought a silk shawl for Chris and one for herself, and some postcards to send home.

On their way again, Felipe took her to a small but exclusive restaurant tucked away in a side street and ordered lunch.

'Relax, Stacy, for goodness' sake. I am not a monster,' he said as she fumbled with her knife and fork.

She looked up at him, startled. 'I am relaxed,' she lied. In actual fact she had been thinking of how the waiter had practically bowed to Felipe when he had taken their order. 'I'm not used to dining in a place like this.'

Felipe leaned across the table, his face disturbingly close to hers. 'I think you are not used to dining with a man,' he countered, looking at her intently.

She coloured under his scrutiny. 'No, you're right, the only man I normally eat with is my father. I'm not as sophisticated as you—or the people you mix with,' she finished, with a spurt of anger. Why did he always have to put her at a disadvantage and make her feel small?

However, when the meal arrived she tucked into it with enjoyment. They had wine to accompany the food and after the third glass Stacy began to feel quite lightheaded.

'More wine?' Felipe asked.

'Oh, no, not for me, I think I've had quite enough,' she replied, covering the top of her glass with her fingers.

'Right, we had better be getting along, then,' Felipe replied.

Back at the car he said, 'We will go to a little beach I know. We can have a rest and a swim later if you like, when we have had time to recover from our meal.'

Stacy agreed. The thought of a lie-down on the beach appealed to her. Her feet felt tired, unused to the heat, and her legs were aching.

They turned off the main road and on to a rugged track which Stacy felt sure couldn't lead anywhere and just as she began to panic they turned a corner and in front of them was the most beautiful beach. She caught her breath and looked at Felipe in wonder.

'You like it?' he enquired.

'It's beautiful,' she replied sincerely.

He stopped the car and leaned across to her. 'Yes, very beautiful,' he repeated, looking at her. He planted a swift kiss on her surprised lips and she jerked away as if she had been stung. Felipe stared at her, the black eyes hardening with annoyance.

'What is the matter with you?' he asked. 'Every time I am anywhere near you you panic. What have I done to make you frightened of me?'

'N—nothing, nothing at all, it's just that—well, I mean, I'm not used to people doing that sort of thing, I haven't . . . oh, never mind,' she finished lamely.

'I do mind. What sort of thing? I haven't done anything—yet,' he said.

Stacy hung her head, unable to reply.

'Stacy, surely you are not trying to tell me that

you have never been kissed before? I will not believe it. You are a beautiful woman, surely you haven't reached this stage in your life without someone making a pass at you?' Felipe queried.

She blushed scarlet. 'I—I've only been out with boys from school, they were not like you. Anyway, you shouldn't ask me such questions.'

He gave an exasperated groan. 'Well, you are right in one respect—I am not like your schoolboys, I am a man. That is the difference, Stacy.'

'Yes,' she agreed, 'that's the difference, and I don't know how to cope with it. Could we go and look at the sea, please?'

Felipe gave an exasperated sigh. He flung open his car door, slammed it shut behind him and began walking towards the sea. Stacy, completely out of her depth, just sat and stared at him. As she watched the broad-shouldered figure walking away from her towards the sea, she wished she had more experience. She wanted to attract him, but knowing that she did put her into a frenzy. Eventually she followed him down to the shoreline, stopping to remove her sandals on the way. Without her heels he seemed even taller, and as she approached he looked down at her.

'I am sorry for my display of bad temper, Stacy. I am not quite sure how to handle you,' he took her hand gently, 'but I intend to find out.'

They walked along the beach as far as they could, and then explored a cave with a natural spring pouring ice cold water down on to the sand. Stacy was surprised that Felipe rolled up his trouser legs, took of his shoes and walked through.

'Oh, it's freezing!' she exclaimed as her sensitive feet touched the icy cold water.

'It comes from within the rocks and is cooled as it

passes through them,' Felipe explained. 'Do you want to swim yet?'

She was feeling rather hot and sticky and a cool dip in the sea was just what she needed, but, hesitant as ever, she stumbled over a decision.

'Er—yes, yes, I think I would. I'll go and fetch my towel,' she told Felipe.

'Don't worry, I will get it for you. Go and have your swim.'

By the time he returned she had shed her clothes and was floating on her back in the buoyant salty water. Stacy was surprised that she could see the bottom even though she was well out of her depth. She heard splashing and looked up to see Felipe heading towards her, cutting through the sea with a swift crawl.

'Well, what do you think of our Mediterranean waters?' he asked her, treading water.

'Much better than the Atlantic any day,' she replied. 'I was told it was smelly and dirty, but this is heaven, so warm, and so clear.'

'Some places are polluted,' he agreed, 'but as yet we are still in control here.'

After a while Stacy made her way back to the beach. The sand was incredibly hot and, finding her towel spread upon the sand, she lay down and closed her eyes against the sun. A few minutes later she heard Felipe do the same, but did not open her eyes.

The next thing she knew was when Felipe bent to touch her shoulder lightly. 'Stacy, I think it is time we were leaving,' he said quietly.

She removed the hat he had placed over her face and stared up at him, unsure of her whereabouts.

'Oh, I'm sorry, I didn't mean to go to sleep,' she apologised.

'You are learning to relax and enjoy yourself, do not apologise. I enjoyed watching you,' Felipe told her, his dark eyes flashing teasingly.

She wasn't sure whether she liked the idea of him watching her while she slept. I could have been snoring, she thought.

'Come—we will go back to the car,' he told her, uncurling himself from beside her. She took his out-stretched hand and he pulled her up with no effort at all. He scooped up the towels and they walked back slowly.

'Stacy, how do you feel about a trip to Bini Beca? It is beautiful by night and there is a little bar which serves enormous king prawns and salad. Would you like to go? I'm sure you would love it.'

'Well,' she said, 'what is Bini Beca?'

'It is a village—designed by an Englishman, by the way. The streets are very narrow, but it is very picturesque and well worth a visit.'

'It sounds nice,' she said, 'but what about Chris, won't she be worried if we are too late?'

'We will go to the house of a friend of mine and ask him if he will let us impose on him to smarten up. I will phone Chris and let her know what is happening. I shall explain to her that I have not abducted you.' He looked at her with amusement in his dark eyes and she felt herself melting.

Stacy laid her dress out in the back of the car and put her handbag on top to stop it from flying away. But she felt it necessary to drape her cardigan across her shoulders. She did not feel adequately covered with just her bikini on.

CHAPTER TWO

AFTER quite a long drive they reached a stretch of road which housed some lovely houses and bungalows, set in landscaped gardens high above the road, and all were painted white.

'Oh, what a lovely place to live!' Stacy exclaimed.

Felipe turned to her and smiled. 'We will soon be at the house of my friend. His name is Juan Cabella,' he told her.

They eventually pulled up a steep driveway and parked outside a delightful white stuccoed bungalow, with a landscaped garden and a fountain in the middle of a small, well cultivated lawn. Stacy got out of the car and looked around at the scene. She did not notice a darkly clad servant open the door, and suddenly a voice broke through her thoughts, but the rush of rapid Spanish was lost on her. Felipe replied and then proceeded to introduce Stacy, in English. Juan Cabella was shorter than Felipe, and stockier, but his eyes appraised the view she afforded with unconcealed pleasure.

'My apologies, *señorita*, I did not realise you were English.' He held out his hand and she shook it. 'I am very pleased to meet you,' he said. 'Fernando has kept your existence very quiet—I did not realise that he possessed such a beautiful sister-in-law. And I notice,' he added, turning to Felipe, 'that you have wasted no time in making her acquaintance.'

'But of course not,' Felipe replied with a shrug.

Juan Cabella apologised for the fact that his wife

32

was out visiting friends, but made them welcome to use his house. They were ushered into a cool hallway with many doors leading from it, left and right. Stacy was shown into an empty bedroom where she took a shower and reapplied her make-up. Her hair was wet, but she knew it would soon dry. She put on her dress, grateful for the cover it afforded, and made her way to the room which Señor Cabella had indicated she should return to. They stood up as she entered and Stacy felt both pairs of eyes upon her as she crossed the room.

'Come and have a drink, *señorita*,' Señor Cabella invited. 'What would you like?'

'I think I'll have a sherry, please—medium,' Stacy replied.

She turned to look at Felipe. He had obviously showered too, his hair was made blacker by water and he looked disturbingly handsome, his chiselled features in profile. He turned and caught her watching him and his intimate smile made her blush.

'I have phoned Chris, she didn't mind at all. She said for you to have a good time.'

'Oh, I'm glad she doesn't mind. I wouldn't like her to worry about me,' Stacy replied.

After a pleasant half hour they again went back to the car and Felipe carefully negotiated the steep drive, while Stacy turned to wave to Señor Cabella, who was watching their departure. As Felipe parked the car a few hundred yards farther up the road, Stacy looked about her in puzzlement. There didn't seem to be anything much to look at and she certainly couldn't see a pub.

'Come on,' said Felipe, 'this way.' He turned down a small alley and Stacy was amazed to find that it was actually a street. She could have touched

the apartments on both sides if she stretched her
arms, out, and the quaintness of the tiny village en-
chanted her. Felipe led her around the maze of small
streets, made colourful with hanging baskets, until
they reached an open space where a small inlet,
dotted with boats, appeared before them. Tiny white
villas curved around the harbour in picturesque
irregularity and Stacy was most impressed. There
were potted flowers outside each door and hanging
baskets of every description containing a multitude
of differing flowers.

'This is called Pueblo de Pescadores,' Felipe told
her. 'The fishermen's village—although it is actually
only used by tourists for their holidays—or at least
most of the accommodation is.'

'It's very pretty,' Stacy replied.

He led her through narrow winding streets where
Stacy could have stretched out her arms and touched
the walls on either side. Minute alleyways led to
other doorways and alcoves of flowers. The streets
were cobbled and awkward to walk on in her high-
heeled sandals, and eventually Felipe led her around
another corner and into a small pub. The sun was
still brilliant outside and the transition from light to
dark temporarily blinded Stacy as she stepped inside.
Felipe guided her to a small table and seated her
before walking over to the bar to order a drink. He
came back with a chilled bottle of wine and two
glasses.

'Would you like the king prawns—or do you
fancy anything else?' he asked.

'Oh no, the king prawns will be fine—with salad,
please, if that's possible.'

'It is indeed,' he replied, rising again from his
chair and going to order.

They had finished one glass of wine each by the time the food arrived. Felipe had been telling Stacy about the building of the village and describing what the area had been like before. The pub was filling up now and it was difficult to see the bar, or the door which they had entered through.

'Ah,' said Felipe, 'our food has arrived.'

They cleared a space on the small table for the enormous plates which held their dinner.

'Oh no, I'll never manage all this!' Stacy groaned.

'Well, just eat what you want and leave the rest,' Felipe reasoned.

He began to ask questions about her life in England and Stacy told him about her father's shop in Birmingham and all about the large city from which she came. It sounded most uninteresting to her ears, considering the sort of life Felipe Cuevas lived, but he nevertheless listened intently to every word she said.

'And what do you think of Menorca?' he asked. 'Would you like to live here?'

'Yes, I'd love to,' Stacy told him. 'But I shouldn't think that's possible. I wouldn't impose on Chris, and I can't speak the language, so I couldn't get a job.'

'Why do you not learn our language?' Felipe asked her.

'I'd like to,' she replied. 'In fact I've been thinking about it already. When I get home I think I'll go to night school and learn.

'Do you live here all the time?' she asked him some moments later, when he had poured her another drink.

'No, I have to go home to Andalusia on occasions.

But I like it here and it is convenient. I am not too far away from my family, but far enough for them not to get in my way.'

Stacy had never heard of Andalusia, but she didn't want to show her ignorance and ask him where it was, so she changed the subject quickly.

'I was really pleased when Chris and Fernando invited me over for a holiday. I've never been abroad before, they waited until I'd finished my exams before sending for me—it was good of them, wasn't it?'

'Indeed it was. Would you like some more wine?'

Stacy shook her head thoughtfully to see if she still felt sober.

'O.K., then, but not too much,' she told him. She knew that the amount she had drunk had already loosened her tongue and she was speaking far more freely than she would normally do.

'I have enjoyed today very much,' Felipe told her. 'It is refreshing to take someone as untried as yourself out for the day. It has been like seeing everything again for the first time.'

'I enjoyed it too,' Stacy replied. 'Thank you very much for bringing me.'

'It was my pleasure. We must do it again in the near future—if your sister does not mind.'

Stacy took another sip of wine, 'I'm sure she wouldn't,' she said.

'Do you mind if I smoke?'

'No, please go ahead.'

He took out a long, thin cheroot and lit it with an expensive-looking lighter, blowing smoke thoughtfully up at the ceiling. Stacy watched him through her lashes. She looked around and noticed some of the women by the bar eyeing him in a similar fashion, and felt proud that it was her company he was keeping. Although he was much older than herself, she was quite aware of his magnetism and good looks. It would not be difficult to get involved with a man like Felipe Cuevas. She jerked her head up quickly when he spoke and flushed darkly at her own thoughts.

'Pardon?'

He leaned closer to her across the table. 'I said, I think it is time I took you home again to your sister, she will be wondering where we've got to.'

Stacy looked down at her watch in surprise. It was almost half past ten. 'Oh, I didn't realise it was so late,' she said lamely, and Felipe laughed.

'It is not late in this part of the world,' he told her, 'it is quite early, but you are not used to such ways and you will be tired soon.'

He took her arm as she stood up and guided her slowly out of the crowded bar. It was very dark outside and they picked their way carefully across the cobbles and back on to the tarmac road. Stacy stumbled over a stone and Felipe quickly steadied her, sending a shiver through her body at his touch.

'Are you all right?' he asked. 'You have not hurt yourself, I hope.'

'No,' she croaked, 'I'm fine, thank you.'

To her disappointment he loosed hold of her and stood looking down into her wide eyes with an unreadable expression.

'We had better get back to the car,' he said almost tersely.

Stacy followed, wondering what was the matter with him. She couldn't help tripping over a stone, after all!

'It's very dark here, isn't it?' she said. 'It's taking

some time for my eyes to adjust from the lights of the bar to this—just as it did when I went from the sunshine into it earlier.'

Felipe turned and took her hand in his, unconscious of the turmoil such an action caused inside her. 'I had better guide you, then,' he said.

'Will you be able to find the way back?' she asked anxiously; she could not recognise anything so far.

'You need not worry,' he replied, 'I shall find my way home. We do not have street lamps here as you do in England.'

He took her slowly back towards the car. Stacy looked up at the clear sky. 'I'm sure there must be far more stars here than there are at home,' she stated, 'I know it's silly, but just look at them—and so bright too. I've never seen so many!'

Felipe laughed, 'They are the same stars, Stacy, it is just that your climate is not as kind to them as ours. Our clean air makes them sparkle.'

He put his arm around her waist and she did not object. In fact she welcomed it. Somewhere in the back of her mind she remembered being frightened of Felipe, but the wine and good food had successfully obliterated that for the moment. It felt curiously safe having his strong arm around her.

Back at the car he opened her door and as she turned to get in he held her back. Turning her towards him, he exerted a gentle pressure on her arms and drew her closer.

'What's the matter?' Stacy asked stupidly.

'What should be the matter?' Felipe replied quietly. 'I have spent a beautiful evening with a beautiful girl and now I want to kiss her. Do you think she will mind?'

Stacy realised that he seemed to be getting closer.

She watched his sensitive mouth with fascination and she liked the feeling it gave her.

'No, I don't think I mind, not at the moment anyway,' she answered truthfully.

'That is good,' he said, drawing her into the circle of his arms as he leaned back against the car. 'Because I want to kiss you very much, and I don't want you to fight me.'

His lips were like a caress on hers to start with, but gradually he began to exert more pressure and she felt her knees beginning to tremble. His arms held her tighter still and suddenly she was aware of the hard length of his body pressing against her own. She shifted position slightly, not realising what it would do to him. He groaned and forced her mouth open with an urgency she did not understand. No one had ever kissed her like that before, and she was carried away with a tide of emotion she had no way of controlling. She found her hands had tangled in the springy hair at the nape of his neck, so tight that her fingers ached. Felipe's hands moulded her to him, sending sensations through her body which she had never experienced before. He began to tremble and Stacy, not aware of his struggle, held him close, her arms around his waist. He kissed her eyelids, her ears, her neck, trailing fire with his lips. She could have denied him nothing, was totally incapable of pulling herself back to normality, but Felipe realised that he could not continue this lovemaking without reaching the point of no return. All his instincts urged him on, but his conscience was proof against them—just. With a stifled groan he held Stacy away from him; his breathing, she noticed, was very laboured and she would have moved closer again if he had let her. He looked into her eyes and saw the confusion mirrored there.

'I am sorry, Stacy, I did not mean to ... You make me lose my head. I am sorry.'

'I don't understand,' she said plaintively.

He took her in his arms again and rested her head against his chest. 'Oh, Stacy, you are such a child! Whatever am I going to do with you?' he said in an anguished voice.

She snuggled closer to him, liking the secure feeling it gave her, but unconscious of her ability to arouse him.

'I—I don't understand,' she repeated. 'What's the matter?'

She looked up at him and as though drawn by a magnet his lips descended to hers again. This time he tried to keep things in a lower key, but Stacy, in her ignorance, did not make it easy for him, so after a brief kiss he released her again, unwilling to torture himself further.

'Stacy, please!' he begged. 'If you do not stop now *I* will not be able to later.'

She looked up at him, confused. 'I don't understand. What have I done wrong?'

He gave a mirthless laugh. 'You have done everything right, that is just the trouble.' He breathed a deep sigh, running a troubled hand through his hair. 'It would not stop at kissing, Stacy, surely you understand that? If I go on any longer you would not be able to stop me when you wanted to. I would have to take you with or without consent.'

'You mean you wanted to make love to me?' she asked innocently.

Felipe let out an exasperated sigh. 'Of course I did—I do. Come, I must get you home. I have done enough damage already.'

'What do you mean? What damage? I liked what you did,' she told him.

'That is not the point,' he snapped. 'Please, Stacy, get in the car.'

Stacy did so. Felipe's rejection of her stung bitterly. She had never behaved in such an abandoned manner in her life before, but with Felipe it had seemed right. Now his attitude had changed so drastically and she could not understand.

'Stop torturing yourself with thoughts, little one, you will only tie yourself in knots. I only do what is best for you—just remember that,' he said, close to her ear.

'I'm afraid it must have been the wine,' she said, looking for something to blame her behaviour on.

'Do not make excuses. It is quite natural for a man and a woman to kiss each other, with or without wine. I wanted to kiss you and you wanted the same, there is nothing wrong with that.'

'Then why are you in a temper?' she asked him.

'Because—oh, Stacy, how can I explain to you? I am like a drowning man who almost reaches a paradise, only to have it snatched away from him by a giant wave. Do you think it was easy for me to let you go?'

She bent her head, her hair falling in curtains around her face to cover her confusion. His hand cupped her chin and turned her around to face him.

'Just accept things as they are for now,' he said. 'Everything will work out right, but we have to have time. You cannot start to run before you walk, as the English say. I have been running for a long time, much longer than you—you are still a child in many ways.'

'I wish you wouldn't keep calling me a child,' Stacy flared. 'I'm sick of being a child!'

'I am sorry, I have spoilt the evening for you—for me as well. I did not mean to do that. Will you forgive me?' Felipe asked, gently massaging her throat with his thumb.

'I suppose so,' she managed, and tried to escape his hold. But Felipe could not resist pulling her into his arms again. He held her head with his hand to stop her moving and made a calculated seduction of her lips which left her gasping, weak and helpless. He looked down into her face, but she was unable to see his expression because it was so dark. He kissed her again, one brief hard kiss, and then moved back to his own side of the car. Stacy felt suddenly bereft.

The powerful engine purred into life and they sped away into the dark night.

'Are you cold?' Felipe asked some moments later.

'Not cold, no. It is going cooler, though, now, isn't it?' she answered.

Felipe stopped the car immediately.

'Where are you going?' she asked.

'Only to fetch you a rug from the trunk.'

He returned with a large red tartan car blanket and handed it to her to wrap around herself. He waited until she was snug and then moved off again. His attitude had changed. He was distant and unapproachable all of a sudden. Stacy did not know how to react. She sat huddled miserably in the corner of her seat berating herself for her lack of experience. The car headlights cut into the darkness in front of them and illuminated the road, but where they did not reach was pitch black. The warmth of the rug and the fact that there was nothing to see made her sleepy and before long she was fast asleep.

Felipe woke her after driving up to the front door of her sister's villa.

'We are home, Stacy, time to wake up,' he told her quietly.

Stacy roused herself and clambered inelegantly from the car.

'Oh, we're here,' she said unnecessarily. 'Thank you very much for a lovely day.'

'It was my pleasure,' Felipe replied. 'I will leave you here. *Buenas noches*.'

With this he turned back to the car, leaving Stacy standing on the steps staring. When the car had pulled out of the drive she pushed open the heavy studded door and went in. Voices could be heard from the lounge, Chris and Fernando, and she wished she could just crawl off to bed without letting them know she was back, but good manners prevailed and she went in. After explaining where they had been she excused herself and left them.

Upstairs in her room she sat on the bed and cried. It had been such a confusing day. After coming out of her shell with Felipe she had been rudely pushed back again. Perhaps people were right, once a man knew he had you where he wanted he lost interest. But he had only kissed her, nothing else. Perhaps she had just been a novelty to him, something different from his usual type of women. He was at least thirty, he must have had plenty of others falling at his feet. Stacy turned her face into the pillow, trying to still these thoughts, and sobbed. How would she be able to face him again?

As it happened it was three days before she saw Felipe again. She and Chris had spent the time sightseeing and browsing around the little shops in Mahón. Fernando had taken them out to a restaurant in Ciudadela for an enormous meal, but in the back of her mind all the time had been Felipe Cuevas. She was spoiling her holiday with thoughts of him. Anger and humiliation fought each other inside her. She had come to visit her sister and brother-in-law—and all she could think about was a virtual stranger. She had decided that when she saw Felipe Cuevas again she would completely ignore him, or, if that was not possible, would remove herself from his presence as quickly as possible.

Chris had been telling her a few things about him which had cemented her decision to keep her distance. She had told Stacy that he was very wealthy and was quite convinced that, because he was rich, he could do exactly as he liked—usually at the expense of others.

'He goes through women at an alarming rate,' Chris had said. 'I hope you don't read anything into him taking you out the other day. It's second nature to him to have a woman hanging on his arm.'

Stacy had hung her head and assured her sister that she had only gone with him to get out of her way.

'That's right, you find yourself a nice English boy—that would be much more suitable for you,' Chris told her. 'The Felipe Cuevases of this world would tie you in knots before you knew where you were.'

'I'm not completely stupid, you know!' Stacy had retorted.

She had been in Cala Galdaña a week; it didn't seem possible. A whole week! She was sitting on the edge of her bed, looking at her reflection in the dressing table mirror. She was much browner now and her hair, naturally light, had been turned into a silvery sheen by the sun. It was time to go to bed, but Stacy felt restless. She wandered around her room, putting things into place, and then leaned out of her window. The sky was dark blue and the stars twinkled in their thousands high above her. There seemed to be no wind and the moon lit up the surroundings.

Putting on a sweater and a pair of jeans, she left her room and went downstairs quietly. There was no sound, the household had gone to bed. She carefully opened the french windows in the lounge and walked out into the garden. She looked up at the stars again, remembering the other occasion when she had noticed them—when she had been to Bini Beca with Felipe—and determinedly pushed the thought to the back of her mind. She walked over the damp lawn and around the flowerbeds. The end of the garden was a sheer cliff, dropping down many feet to the shimmering bay below. There was only a waist-high stone wall protecting her from the precipice and she leaned on it confidently, listening to the almost deafening sound of the crickets all around her.

The sand looked almost white in the brilliance of the moonlight and the sound of the sea lapping against the sand and the tinkling of the rigging on the many yachts moored below could just be heard. Stacy sighed heavily and brushed her hair away from her face.

Only three more weeks and she would have to go home; to try, along with everyone else, to get a job. Would she be able to afford another holiday like this? She doubted it. Chris wouldn't be allowed to pay again; it wasn't fair, even if Fernando was rich.

Suddenly she was startled by a sound behind her and she turned quickly, gasping at the dark figure looming up beside her.

'Who is it?' she squeaked.

'It is only me—Felipe,' replied a well remembered voice. 'I am sorry if I startled you, Stacy.'

'Startled me?' she replied angrily. 'I could have fallen over the cliff! And what are you doing in Chris's garden? Haven't you got one of your own to prowl around?'

Stacy made to walk past him, but he stepped into her path.

'My, my, I did not know you possessed such a temper! What is the matter?'

'Matter? Nothing's the matter. I come out here for a peaceful walk and find you here lurking about, that's all. Now if you don't mind, I'd like to go.' She pushed at the hard chest in front of her, but as she expected it did not budge. She tried to dodge round him, but he caught her wrist and held on.

'Let me go!' she shouted.

'Not until you tell me why you are so angry; and please do not shout, do you want to wake everyone up?' he asked her quietly.

'Let me go, I said! I have nothing to say to you, you have no right to keep me here,' Stacy whispered furiously.

'Why are you so angry?' he repeated. 'You did not find my company unpleasant the other night.'

She tried to hit him, but he easily countered her blow.

'Well, I do now,' she snapped.

'That is a pity, because I do not intend to let you go just yet. I want to know what is wrong,' Felipe told her. He took hold of her shoulders and turned her to face him. 'Is it because I have neglected you for a while, hmmm?' he asked.

'I came here to see my sister and her husband,'

she replied icily. 'It doesn't matter whether you are around or not.'

'Oh dear, I have upset you, haven't I? I did have a good reason, you know,' he told her.

'Please, I'm not interested in your reasons. I want to go to bed—now loose hold of me,' she begged.

'That is a tantalising thought,' he said, ignoring her last words. 'I would also like to go to bed, but I would like to take you with me.'

Stacy struggled furiously with him. 'How dare you speak to me like that! What do you think I am?'

Felipe laughed quietly. 'I know exactly what you are, *querida*,' he told her. 'That is why I have not . . . why I have kept away from you. I do not usually want to go around defiling innocents.'

As she continued to struggle his grip on her arms became tighter until it hurt and she was forced to stop. Her face was mutinous, and he threw back his head and laughed.

'Oh, Stacy!' he sighed, shaking his head and drawing her determinedly towards him.

She dug her heels into the ground in an effort to thwart him, even though she knew it was futile. As she came closer he fastened his strong hands around her waist, still staring down at her with an inscrutable expression on his face. 'Please,' she begged.

'Yes,' he replied, 'please—please me.' He jerked her closer to him until she could feel the whole length of him against her. She began to tremble again, remembering their last contact. Then she struggled frantically, remembering her resolution to avoid him.

'You would be advised to stop struggling, Stacy. You do not know what you are inciting,' Felipe's voice broke through her frenzy. He bent his head as she opened her mouth to speak and captured her lips with his. Stacy tried to remain still and cold while he bombarded her with kisses, but when his hands began to move possessively over her she could feel her traitorous body responding. He lifted her sweater and caressed the smooth skin of her back. She arched herself closer to him, her hands gripping the belt at the back of his trousers.

'Oh, Stacy,' he murmured in her ear, his breath sending shivers through her, 'you do not know how much I have longed to do this over the past few days—it has been agony.'

He buried his face in the hollow of her neck; he obviously needed a shave, Stacy thought, as his hair-roughened chin acted like an abrasive against her soft skin. It was not an unpleasant sensation, though.

'Why did you stay away, then?' she asked.

'I do have work to do, you know,' he chided. 'But also, I do not trust myself with you. I am no angel, Stacy, I have always been able to take what I want and not count the cost. But you are different. I want you badly, but I cannot take advantage of your innocence.'

She pressed herself to him, unable to think of a reply. She felt his muscles jerk in response to her touch.

'For God's sake Stacy, don't!' he pleaded.

'Why not?' she queried. 'I thought you liked it.'

'I like it too much,' he replied huskily, bending his head and fastening his lips to hers in a hard, passionate kiss. His hands searched over her relentlessly, turning her legs to jelly. He lifted her sweater over her breasts and bent to kiss them.

'You do not wear a bra,' he stated unnecessarily,

his voice almost unrecognisable.

'No, not very often,' she told him.

'I'm glad,' he said, feathering his lips across the hardening peaks.

She heard a low moan which she couldn't believe came from herself. Felipe lifted her off her feet and lowered her to the damp earth. He immediately came down on top and for the first time she felt the whole weight of his body crushing hers beneath it. There was something decidedly sensuous in that contact, and she arched herself against him to try and get even closer. He took her lips again and she could scarcely breathe. Her hands parted his shirt and she pulled it from the waistband of his trousers and ran her hands around his back, feeling him tremble above her.

'Oh God, Stacy, I want you so much,' he whispered against her mouth. '*Te quiero.*'

'Felipe,' she replied in a strangled voice, at that moment quite willing to give in to any demand he made of her.

Suddenly he raised his head from hers and pulled down her sweater, rolling over on to his back. He gave a stifled cry and covered his face with his hands.

'Dear God, what am I doing?' he agonised.

Stacy, suddenly bereft, tried to control the trembling of her body. She ached with longings she did not understand, but she knew that only Felipe could assuage them. She was now aware of the damp earth beneath her and the chillness of the wind across the water. She looked across at him and burst into tears. Sobbing uncontrollably, she heard him move and felt his strong hands grasp her shoulders.

'Stacy, please, don't do that—please stop.'

'I can't,' she spluttered.

He stood and pulled her up beside him, putting his arms around her and resting her head on his chest. 'Stacy, *amada*, you must stop, you will make yourself ill. Come with me,' he said. He urged her across the grass and over a low stone wall into his own garden. Stacy was too drained to protest, allowing him to lead her like a lost sheep. He took her to a spacious lounge, tastefully and expensively decorated, but Stacy was in no mood to appreciate it. She had calmed down sufficiently by this time, but misery had been replaced by anger and humiliation at his treatment of her and the way she had indulged him.

'Sit down,' he ordered, and she obeyed unthinkingly.

Felipe went to a low sideboard and extracted a bottle and two glasses from it. 'Drink this,' he said after pouring a generous measure into each glass.

'I don't want it,' Stacy replied sullenly. She turned her face from him, knowing what a sight she must look with a blotchy face and red eyes.

'I didn't ask you if you wanted it,' he replied, 'I said drink it.' He forced the glass into her hand and up to her lips and she was obliged to drink the fiery brandy before it ran down her chin and into her lap.

'Wait here,' said Felipe, striding out of the room. He was only away a few seconds and when he returned he was carrying an Aran sweater.

'Take off your wet sweater and put this on. If you do not I might be tempted to do it for you.'

Stacy took the proffered sweater and turned her back to him as she eased her own damp one over her head.

She heard his sharp intake of breath and hurried

to cover herself with his sweater, but before she could manoeuvre herself into it she felt his hands encircle her waist from behind. She struggled to be free of him, but he held her tightly and refused to let go.

'Stacy, I have told you before, stop struggling.' He pulled her back against him and rested his head on top of hers. She waited, wondering what would happen next, but he remained still, just holding her. After what seemed like hours he released her, and a sense of disappointment crept over her like a wave.

'Cover yourself up,' he said quietly, 'and come and sit down. I want to talk to you, and I can't think straight with you in that state of undress.'

Stacy obediently pulled the soft sweater over her head; it was far too big for her and she had to push the sleeves up to uncover her hands. She looked over to where Felipe was sitting, watching her.

'What do you want to talk about?' she asked with an air of nonchalance she did not feel.

'Come and sit down. Do not try to play games with me—you will only lose,' Felipe told her.

'Huh,' Stacy replied, 'don't I know it!' But she went forward anyway and sat on the sofa, at the opposite end to Felipe.

He shook his head and moved closer to her. She looked up into the dark eyes which were in shadow in the dimly lit room.

'What?' she asked impatiently.

'You are very beautiful,' he replied evenly. 'When I see you I cannot keep my hands off you. But I have great respect for your sister and her husband and for you also, and I cannot—my conscience will not let me do what my body cries out for. It is agony to let you go when I need you so badly, especially when I know that, because of your innocence, you would willingly let me continue.'

'Felipe!' she protested, embarrassed by the turn of the conversation.

'Let me continue,' he cut in. 'For once in my life I have had to exercise restraint. I must admit I do not like it. I would like you to have been a little older, a little more worldly-wise—not for my sake, necessarily, but for yours. You know nothing of life— you are too young for me. All these things I know, and yet I do not want to think of them. I am confused.'

'Felipe, listen,' Stacy begged. 'I know I'm green, you don't have to tell me that. I've lived a very sheltered life, I suppose. You overwhelm me, I haven't met anyone like you before. But I know that when other people have made passes at me they turned me cold, repulsed me even. But with you it's different. I don't feel repulsed. It's—good,' she trailed off, looking up into his eyes and seeing the expression on his face.

Felipe took her hand and squeezed it. His other hand trailed down the side of her face and across her lips, and Stacy shuddered involuntarily and leaned closer to him. Felipe pulled her into the circle of his arms and held her close. 'I think we must get to know each other better. I want to marry you.' He held her fast as she struggled to look up at him, but he kept her face against his chest. 'But first of all I want to find out whether you would be content with me, because, be sure, once I had you I would never let you go. You would be mine for ever, no turning back.'

'Oh, Felipe,' she stammered, 'I'm sure that's all I'll ever want. I can't imagine ever wanting anything but you.'

'At this moment you probably can't,' he replied gravely, 'but you have never spread your wings, *pequeña*. Once we were married it would be too late to spread them anywhere but over me. I want you to be happy, and I have to give you a chance of finding out.'

'Don't send me away, Felipe,' Stacy begged him. 'I should be so miserable!'

He stood up, releasing her. 'Well, for the moment, *querida*, you will have to be miserable—and so shall I. It is very late and I must send you back to the safety of your family. But God knows, I wish I could take you with me to my bed.' He bent and pulled her up off the sofa. 'Come along, this situation is far too intimate for my peace of mind.'

'But, Felipe,' she pleaded, 'what are we going to do?'

He turned to her and placed his hands on her shoulders.

'Tomorrow I will come to the pool, early, and we will have a swim—under the watchful eyes of your dear sister, I hope. I shall ask her permission to take you out tomorrow night, but this time we will go to a place where there are plenty of people and you do not tempt me to fall for your charms. I must think, but now I am far too tired.'

'But. . . .' Stacy began.

Felipe put a finger to her lips. 'No—I am the first man who has stirred your senses, but you must think of the consequences before you rush into this relationship. I have been through it all already—you have not even started.'

Stacy felt her anger rise, she stamped her foot impatiently.

'Why won't you listen to me? I'm not a baby, I

know what I like and what I don't!'

Felipe took her hand again and pulled her un-ceremoniously out of the door and across the lawns. He stopped at the french windows and looked down at her.

'You have an English saying—marry in haste, repent at leisure—you would do well to think on it for a while. I will see you tomorrow morning.'

He bent and kissed her hard on the lips. She immediately put her arms around his neck and pulled him closer. She felt a tremor pass through him and an increasing pressure from his mouth, but almost immediately he dragged himself away from her, but keeping hold of her hands.

'Goodnight, Stacy, sweet dreams,' he said quietly and with that he turned on his heel and strode away. Stacy stared after his retreating back until he was swallowed up in the darkness, then she squeezed through the windows and back through the lounge. She tiptoed up the stairs and into her room, closing the door silently behind her. She looked down at the Aran sweater she was wearing and fingered the soft wool; it looked hand-knitted. She thought of her own sweater lying in a heap on Felipe's carpet, and wondered what his housekeeper would make of that! Felipe . . . could he really want to marry her? And if he did, why all the drama about waiting? She flopped down on the bed, confused and tired.

The sun was streaming through a chink in the curtains. Stacy turned over and looked at her alarm clock. Seven-thirty. She threw back the bedcovers and padded across to the bathroom. After a quick shower she selected a skimpy white bikini from her wardrobe and teamed it up with a red floral wrap-over skirt. She combed her hair until it shone and pinned one side back with a comb, leaving the other side to fall gently around her face. Pleased with the effect, she swung happily away from the mirror and went downstairs.

Chris was in the kitchen talking to Señora Sanchez and Stacy went to join them.

'Good morning,' she said brightly.

'My, my, you look a picture this morning!' Chris commented, eyeing her appearance. 'You look as though you've stepped off the cover of a magazine.'

'Thanks,' Stacy replied. 'It's all this good life I'm getting used to. I think it suits me. Apart from Daddy, there's nothing I've missed about England since I came.'

'Well,' Chris replied lightly, 'you'll have to find yourself a nice Menorcan to keep you here in the style to which you're becoming accustomed.'

'Mmmmm—what a good idea,' Stacy replied 'not a bad idea at all.'

'Well, walk around like that for long and I'm sure you'll have dozens of offers,' Chris laughed. She picked up their breakfast tray which Señora Sanchez had just prepared and Stacy followed her out into the garden.

The sun was already quite hot and they drank their iced fruit juice appreciatively. A short while later Felipe appeared through the bushes at the side of the pool. He was only wearing swimming trunks and Stacy's heart began to beat so fiercely that she was sure they would be able to hear it. She watched him through her lashes as he walked with easy grace up the path towards them. As he reached them his smile encompassed them both, but Stacy felt his eyes linger on her and then travel the length of her body.

'*Buenas dias,* ladies,' he greeted casually. 'It is a beautiful morning, is it not?'

'Hi, Felipe,' Chris greeted him, quite at ease, unlike Stacy.

'Hello,' she said, and was surprised by the strangled tone of her voice.

'I must say,' Felipe continued, 'that you both look delectable this morning. It is enough to make a man lose his head—two beautiful women at the breakfast table. Fernando is a lucky man.'

'Hey,' Chris chided playfully, 'what's all this buttering up for—you're not trying to wheedle an invitation to dinner, are you, because if so you know you only have to ask.'

Felipe held his hand up to his brow. 'Women—they are so suspicious! If I pay you a compliment it is because it is true.'

'Here,' said Chris, pouring out a glass of fruit juice for him, 'drink this before I push you in the pool!'

'Heartless,' he grinned. 'Women are heartless, no sense of romance at all.' He sipped his drink, his eyes fastening on Stacy's over the rim of the glass. She tried to look back at him steadily, but found it too difficult and looked out over the blue-tinted water to the cliffs beyond.

'What are you intending today?' Felipe asked. 'Because if you are not already committed I would like to take you out on the boat.'

'Oh,' Chris clapped her hands together, her red hair flying, 'that would be lovely!'

At that point Fernando appeared through the french windows, dressed casually, Stacy noticed—he obviously wasn't working today.

'Ah, Felipe,' he said, taking a seat next to his wife and dropping his arm across her shoulders, 'you are an early bird this morning. Where have you been hiding—we haven't seen you for almost a week?'

'Oh, business,' Felipe shrugged. 'I was just commenting upon the beauty of your two lovely ladies, but for my trouble I get threatened with a dip in the pool by your wife. There is no justice!'

Fernando laughed. 'I am inclined to agree with you.'

'Felipe has offered to take us out on the boat today, Fernando. Can we go, please?' Chris chipped in, looking at her husband appealingly.

'Well, of course,' he replied. 'I take it that I am included in the invitation,' he smiled at his friend, 'or was it your intention to whisk them away on your own?'

'Oh no, of course you are included. I think I need help to control them,' Felipe replied.

'I don't think you would have much trouble,' Fernando told him, 'I have never seen you lose control of anything.'

Felipe smiled, deliberately looking at Stacy. 'There is always a first time,' he said meaningfully.

Stacy could feel a rush of colour flood her face and she bent down and adjusted the strap of her sandal.

'Well,' Felipe's deep voice concluded, 'in that case I will have a quick dip and go back to get ready.' His head appeared under the table, where Stacy was putting the finishing touches to her sandal strap.

'Make sure you wear flat-soled shoes, Stacy,' he advised her. 'The deck becomes too hot to walk on when the sun is high. And bring a thick sweater too. If we stay out late it will become quite cold on the water.' His dark eyes held a hint of mischief. He knew why she had dived under the table.

She raised her head and sat up. 'Right, I'll do that,' she said in an even voice. 'I don't think I'll have a swim this morning. I'll wait until we get to the sea.'

'Then I shall take a lonely swim around your pool, if I may, Chris?' he said, and after removing his sandals headed for the water.

Chris and Fernando started to discuss what they would take with them, and Stacy watched the darkly tanned figure dive into the water with hardly a splash and then break into a strong crawl across the pool.

Soon afterwards they all returned indoors to get ready. Stacy decided to leave on what she was wearing. She had noticed Felipe's appraisal of her earlier and knew he liked the way she looked. It was strange, she had never bothered to dress specifically for anyone but herself before. To dress to impress someone else opened up a whole new horizon to her. She packed a spare bikini, a pair of jeans and a thick sweater. Felipe had not mentioned her own damp one which she had left on his lounge floor.

An hour later they were unpacking the car at Cala Galdaña beach and walking across the hot sand to a small dinghy which Felipe had taken to the water. A picnic basket and a cooler bag were loaded into it, along with the rugs and sweaters; Felipe made the first trip out to the yacht on his own to open the hatches and let the fresh air in before the others came aboard. In all he made three journeys before they were all aboard.

Stacy was fascinated. The yacht was much bigger than she had imagined. It looked much smaller from the shore. Down a small flight of steps was a sumptuous cabin. It was fitted with dark blue Draloncovered seats and on the floor was thick-piled carpet. There were plenty of teak lockers for storage. Felipe showed her the galley; although it was quite small it was nevertheless fitted with every modern convenience, food mixer, waste disposal unit, split level cooker, even an electric can-opener.

'They came with the boat,' Felipe told her. 'I would not have bothered to install them myself.'

'Oh, don't apologise,' said Chris. 'I'm sure Stacy doesn't begrudge you life's little luxuries.'

'I think it's lovely,' Stacy said, looking eagerly around her. 'Just like a big doll's house.'

Felipe laughed. 'Is that how you see it? I have never thought of it like that.'

'A pretty expensive doll's house, darling,' Chris replied.

He then showed them the bathroom, which was also well equipped but compact. It looked cool and fresh—all pale lemon.

There were six berths—two double cabins and two single. Their decor was excellent, and again there were lockers fitted into every conceivable space for storage. Stacy wished that Felipe and Chris would go away so that she could explore on her own. She wanted to mooch around unhindered, looking in every cupboard and drawer, not because she was particularly interested in their contents—just because she was fascinated by it all.

She imagined Felipe and herself travelling to far-off places aboard the boat when they were married, and had to turn away to hide the excited smile which threatened to overtake her. She didn't want Chris to see her inner thoughts.

'Do you like it?' Felipe asked, his dark eyes watching her closely. 'I love it,' she replied. 'You're very lucky to own something as beautiful as this.'

Felipe nodded thoughtfully. It appeared to Stacy that he had never thought of that before.

'Yes,' he said, 'I suppose I am.'

'Are we going to stay down here talking all day, Felipe? Or are you going to take us out? Fernando is itching to take a turn at the wheel.'

'But of course, Chris,' Felipe replied, indicating that they should precede him back up to the bridge.

'Impressed?' Chris asked as Felipe went to join Fernando.

'Of course—who wouldn't be?'

'Yes, exactly,' her sister replied. 'Come on, let's go and sit in the sunshine.'

They walked towards the bows where there was a sundeck and sat on the sun-loungers scattered there.

'Why don't they put the sails up?' Stacy asked.

'Because it's too much trouble, darling. It needs a crew to sail under canvas. It's much easier to use the engines.'

'Well,' Stacy said reasonably, 'there isn't much wind about today anyway.'

Chris lay back and closed her eyes, but Stacy felt restless. She wanted to be with Felipe. Eventually she crept away and went to join Felipe and Fernando on the bridge.

She stood looking back at the bay as they moved seaward through the cliffs on either side which sheltered the enormous bay. There were pine trees surrounding the golden crescent of sand, and Stacy could see an old green bus labouring its way up the winding road from the beach.

'Well, what do you think of my toy? Do you like my *Gaviota*?' a deep voice asked near her ear. Stacy was afraid to turn around, he was so close behind her.

'It's beautiful, absolutely,' she answered sincerely. 'What does *Gav—Gaviota* mean?'

'It means seagull. You look very beautiful too, you know,' he told her, kissing her neck just below her ear.

'Don't,' she pleaded, 'Chris will see you.'

'They are too busy guiding the yacht out of the bay at the moment,' he replied. 'And anyway, what difference does it make—they will know soon enough.'

His hand slid around her bare midriff and she shuddered with the contact. He had removed his towelling shirt and the touch of his hair-roughened chest against her arm made her tingle. The dark curly hairs which grew down to his navel tickled and she lifted her hand to rub her other arm. It came into contact with Felipe and he caught hold of it and turned her around. She tried to wriggle it out of his grasp, but he would not let go. Stacy looked round frantically to see if Chris and Fernando could see, but realised that they were out of sight. She looked up into his eyes which were full of amusement at her behaviour.

He bent his head and took her mouth, softly, then with increasing pressure. He let her go quite suddenly and she stood dazed, her senses still swimming madly.

'I dare not go on,' he whispered in her ear. 'I might not want to stop.' He took Stacy's hands and held them tightly. 'I have been waiting for that all morning,' he confessed. 'Now, let us go and see where they are taking us,' he added, pulling her behind him.

They sailed slowly around the island, taking in

the rugged coastline, dotted with pine trees. Stacy
was fascinated by the flying fish which took to the
air as the boat disturbed them. The water was such
a deep blue and even though it was deep she marvelled at the fact that the bottom was still clearly
visible.

Before they ate lunch they all went for a swim,
jumping over the side of the boat into the clear,
warm water. This gave them an excellent appetite
for the cold chicken and salad, savoury flan and
gâteau which Felipe's housekeeper had prepared for
their lunch. This was followed by huge fresh peaches
which had them all laughing at each other as they
squirted juice everywhere.

In the afternoon they lay out on the deck and
sunbathed. Stacy, as usual, fell asleep, and was unaware that Felipe lifted her gently into his arms and
carried her down to one of the tiny bedrooms below
and deposited her on top of the covers to sleep out of
the glare of the sun. He stood looking down at her
for some time before running his hands through his
hair and turning sharply away and back up the steps
to the deck.

It was two hours later when she awoke, bemused
by the gently rocking motion beneath her and the
unfamiliar surroundings. She swung her legs off the
bed and stood up. The slight noise must have attrac-
ted Felipe's attention as he walked in at that
moment.

'Ah, so the Sleeping Beauty awakes. I was beginning to think I was going to have to spend the
afternoon with only myself for company.'

'Where are Chris and Fernando?' she asked.

'They, like you, are taking a siesta, but unlike you
they have only just begun,' he replied.

'Oh, I didn't really intend to go to sleep. I always seem to when I lie in this sun—how did I get down here?'

'I carried you, very carefully so as not to wake you. Don't you think that was clever in such a confined space?' he asked. 'I didn't want you to get sunburned.' He stepped closer, his fingers tracing her jawbone. 'I would not like to see your skin red and sore. I like to see it glowing like it is now.' His voice was getting noticeably thicker and Stacy swayed towards him, willing him to come closer still.

He needed no second bidding and wrapped his arms around her, pressing her down the length of his body. She had never been so close to him before with so few clothes on, and the effect of his warm skin on hers started her legs trembling. Felipe could feel it, she knew, and he caught her to him, lifting her feet off the floor and placing her back on to the bed. She did not take her arms from around his neck and with a muffled groan he came down beside her, trapping her legs with his.

'Stacy,' he groaned hoarsely, 'this is madness!' But even so he rolled on top of her, the weight of his body a potent stimulant as it pressed hers down into the softness of the bed.

She wrapped her arms tighter around his neck, glorying in the feel of his warm, strong body. He began to kiss her fiercely and once again she felt a tide of longing sweep through her. Eventually, when they were both gasping for breath, he broke away and buried his face in the hollow between her neck and shoulder.

'Oh, Stacy, I do not think I can wait for you much longer. I wanted to give you time to get used to the idea, give you a chance to change your mind, but I do not think I am capable of holding back, I need you too much.'

'I want to be with you,' Stacy told him hoarsely. 'I've never felt this way about anyone before. I don't need anything else, this is all I'll ever want.'

'I fear I am too old for you,' Felipe said harshly. 'My head tells me so, but my body most certainly does not.'

'That's stupid, of course you're not too old. If you love someone enough that sort of thing is immaterial,' Stacy reasoned.

Felipe looked down into her eyes. 'And do you love me, I wonder? Or am I a new experience for you, nothing more?'

'No!' she cried. 'How dare you suggest such a thing! You think I go around doing this sort of thing just for the experience?'

He laughed. 'Of course not. Do not lose your temper, or I might find it necessary to restrain you—and I can think of many ways which would be most enjoyable.'

Stacy gazed into his eyes and as he looked down at her she noticed that his were almost black with passion. She raised her hand to touch his cheek and he turned his lips to her palm, his tongue tickling its sensitivity.

'Very well, I give in,' he said resignedly. 'When your father comes over I shall ask his permission to marry you. If he agrees, we will be married as soon as possible. I do not want to wait much longer for you—I do not want to wait at all.'

'Then why wait?' she whispered, astounded at her own temerity.

He lifted himself up from her with a quizzical expression. 'Temptress!' he accused. 'You would like me to make love to you with your sister and her husband asleep above us? I could just imagine what would happen if they were to awake and find us so—I imagine they would fall into the water with shock! No, for once in my life I will do it properly. I think you deserve that much, *amada*.'

Stacy sat up and looked at him, grateful but disappointed. 'All right, if that's what you want.'

'It is what is right,' he corrected.

'I'm sure Daddy will be surprised that both Chris and I have chosen foreign men. He'll have a shock when he knows how quickly all this has happened.'

'Yes,' replied Felipe thoughtfully. 'He is in for many shocks, I think. And now,' he changed the subject abruptly, 'I think it is time we thought about making our way around the rest of the island finding ourselves a nice little place for dinner. We will be hungry soon, I think.'

'Right,' Stacy replied.

They made their way back to the deck and found Chris and Fernando awake.

'Where have you two been hiding?' Chris asked.

'I've been fast asleep,' Stacy told her. 'Felipe came down when he heard me moving about.'

Felipe looked at Stacy, then at the couple lying at their feet. 'Shall we tell them, Stacy?' he asked.

She nodded her head, not taking her eyes off him. Chris, sensing something important sat up abruptly, shielding her eyes with her hand.

'I have asked Stacy to marry me,' Felipe said in a quiet, even voice.

'And I've accepted,' Stacy interrupted before anyone could say anything.

Chris's mouth gaped open and Fernando sat up saying, '*What?*'

Chris was the first to recover. 'How did all this happen?—we didn't even know. Well, I knew you'd taken a fancy to her, Felipe, but ... this is so sudden.'

'Come,' Felipe commanded, 'we will have a drink, it will help you recover from the shock.'

They all trooped down to the cabin—it seemed very dark after the bright glare of the sun. Felipe, the only person who seemed quite at ease, as though nothing had happened, opened a locker and produced bottles of whisky and mixers.

'What will you have? There are other things if you don't want whisky.'

Fernando opted for straight whisky, Chris and Stacy both had whisky and dry. Felipe had a liberal helping and sat down next to Stacy on a low divan.

Chris, obviously having sorted her thoughts out, said, 'Oh, Stacy, I'm very happy for you. Apart from Fernando, who you can't have because he's mine, I can't think of a nicer person in the world than Felipe. I'm sure things could be really good between you. And you, Felipe, what can I say? She's my sister and I love her, I think you've made an excellent choice. Her head won't be turned by material things—she likes people for themselves.' She went over to them and kissed them both on the cheeks.

Fernando, still shocked by the announcement, said, 'I too am thrilled, but stunned. I did not even know you had ... well ... how did this happen?'

'I just knew from the moment I saw her that she was someone special,' Felipe told his friend candidly.

'I hope she can cope with you and all the pressures you work under,' Fernando began, but Felipe waved his words aside and diverted the conversation along another channel.

A bottle of champagne was produced and they all drank each other's health and happiness until the bottle was finished. Stacy was carried along with the conversation, but she was not really listening. She had been worried about the reaction Felipe's words would cause, but Fernando had seemed genuinely happy for them. Chris she wasn't so sure about. Nevertheless she was glad it was out in the open at last and she could talk about it freely.

It was eight o'clock by the time they got under way again and a chill had settled on the water. Stacy donned her sweater, feeling as though she was walking three feet above the ground. She went up to the helm and stood next to Felipe as he guided the yacht into the port of Mahón. There were islands on both sides. Felipe pointed to one in the middle of the harbour.

'That is the Isla del Rey, the hospital island, and that one was used as a quarantine island. People who wanted to enter Menorca had to pass through there before they could be admitted. Over there you can see the remains of the fortress of San Felipe. It was completed by the British, by the way, when they occupied the island in the eighteenth century.' He pointed up the cliffs to a colonial style building high above them. 'That is Golden Farm,' he said. 'Legend has it that Admiral Lord Nelson spent some time there when he came to Menorca—he brought his Lady Hamilton with him. That one over the other side there was the home of Admiral Lord Collingwood.'

'You're a mine of information, aren't you?' Stacy said teasingly. 'You're better than a guided tour. Where did you learn all this from?'

'Oh, I am interested in the history of the places where I live—it makes them much more interesting. I am not boring you, am I?'

'Oh no, I'm fascinated. I could listen to you talking for hours and not get bored.'

'I am glad to hear it,' Felipe replied, kissing the tip of her nose.

'I didn't even know Nelson had been to Menorca,' Stacy told him.

'Ah, then I have taught you something. Nelson only came here once, for a short visit. It was supposedly he who gave us the traditional recipe for our Mahón gin—it is made with lemons instead of the usual oranges. There, that is something else I am sure you did not know.'

'I've learned a lot of things since I came to Menorca,' she told him meaningfully.

Felipe turned to her and took her face between his hands. 'I am glad I am the one who has taught you, *querida*.'

'Mmmmm, so am I,' she replied as he gently kissed the tip of her nose.

'We will find a little secluded restaurant—nothing elaborate—we are not dressed for it. Otherwise I could have taken you to the Yacht Club,' Felipe said.

'I don't mind where we go,' Stacy replied. 'I'd be happy to eat fish and chips out of newspaper!'

Felipe laughed. 'That is one of the things about you that I love, you are not impressed by glamour. That is very rare nowadays—or so I have found.' He kissed her swiftly before turning his attention to bringing in the boat.

They ate an excellent meal in a tiny restaurant, small, but the food was delicious and the service impeccable. They were all in a lighthearted mood and the meal was interspersed with happy laughter. Feeling replete, they made their way back to the yacht after walking along the quay and looking at the large ships docked alongside. Darkness was closing in and it was necessary to use lights to guide the yacht back into Cala Galdaña Bay.

They unloaded the boat and packed their empty food hampers into the car. Felipe handed Fernando the keys, saying, 'I am going to make Stacy work for her passage. I am taking her up the difficult way—if you don't mind, that is?'

'No, of course not,' Fernando laughed. 'I trust you to take care of her.' He turned to Stacy. 'I hope you are not too tired, *cara*, Felipe is a hard man to make you walk up so many steps.'

'Steps—what steps?' she queried.

'Come,' said Felipe, taking her hand, 'I will show you. We will see you back at the villa shortly; we will probably need a drink—*adios*.'

They walked across the now cool sand towards the cliffs. Stacy had not noticed before, not having been on the beach in the dark, that there was a zig-zag of lights working its way up the cliff face ahead of them.

'Is that the way we're going?' she asked.

'Yes, I hope so,' Felipe replied, 'Do you feel up to it—it is quite a steep climb?'

'Of course I do,' she answered, willing to walk anywhere as long as she could be with Felipe. 'We can't see this from the villa,' she commented.

'No, it is beneath the line of vision—the cliff overhangs.'

The steps seemed to get steeper and steeper as they ascended. They stopped at intervals and looked out over the bay at the winking lights of the beach bars and the reflection of the moon on the water.

'Oh, Felipe, everything is so beautiful, I can't believe this is happening to me,' Stacy sighed.

'You had better believe it,' he replied, kissing her gently. 'Stacy, there are things we must discuss, not right now, of course, but we must talk. You know nothing about me . . .'

'I know I love you,' she replied earnestly, 'what more do I need to know? You aren't married, are you?'

'Of course not,' Felipe exclaimed.

'Well, that's O.K., then. I'd die if I found out you were married. Come on, we'd better get moving or Chris will wonder what's going on.'

He chuckled, 'I think she would have a good idea!'

They continued up the steps until they reached the top, both out of breath with the effort.

'Whew!' exclaimed Stacy. 'I don't think I'd want to do that again in a hurry!'

'It is good for the leg muscles,' Felipe replied.

'Tell me that another time, I don't think my leg muscles agree with you at the moment,' she said, laughing up at him.

He leaned against the high stone wall that bordered the cliff top and drew her into the circle of his arms. The only sound was the constant chirruping of crickets and occasionally a rustle of a small lizard disturbing the dry grass.

They arrived back at the villa to find Chris and Fernando having a drink in their comfortable lounge.

'Ah,' said Fernando as they entered, 'come and have a drink—I should think you are in need of one—what would you like?'

'I'll have a sherry,' said Stacy.

Felipe decided on brandy and they sat down with their drinks and relaxed after their exertion. It was very late when Felipe left. He turned and gave Stacy a long hard kiss, obviously determined to keep his head, and then left. Stacy went off to bed in a state of euphoria.

The following day Felipe had a business appointment, but he had promised to take Stacy to a jewellers to buy a ring. She awoke early and hurriedly showered and dressed, spending extra time over her light make-up and brushing her hair. She went down to breakfast humming happily to herself.

Chris had not surfaced yet, but Señora Sanchez was in the kitchen making coffee.

'*Buenas dias*,' she smiled at Stacy.

'*Buenas dias*, Chezzie, it's a beautiful morning, isn't it!'

'Ah, *si*, bootiful,' she repeated, raising her hands in the air in a typically Latin gesture. 'You wish breakfast?'

'Mmmm, I'm starving,' Stacy replied.

'You sit in the *jardín*, I will bring,' Chezzie told her in her heavy accented English.

The sun was very bright and Stacy needed to put on her sunglasses to shield her eyes. The garden smelled fresh and heavily perfumed and Stacy took deep lungfuls of air, breathing in the sweetness. Chris came out almost immediately and joined her at the table. She put the tray containing their breakfast down and sat on the chair opposite.

'I met Chezzie coming out,' she explained. 'You're up bright and early, couldn't you sleep?'

'Oh yes, I slept very well, but I woke up early—it

was too nice to stay in bed,' Stacy replied, pouring out some fresh orange juice.

Chris was looking at her across the table. 'I'm very happy for you, of course, Stacy, really I am. I know how it felt when I met Fernando. But are you sure? You only met Felipe a short while ago. Don't go rushing into things, will you, until you're absolutely certain.'

'Of course I'm certain,' Stacy replied. 'Anyway, you can talk—look at you and Fernando! You wouldn't actually say you'd known him all that long before you decided to marry. You only met him on the last week of your holidays!'

Chris laughed. 'Touché! It's just that you're my little sister and I don't want to see you get hurt.'

Stacy picked up a roll and buttered it before replying. 'Felipe wouldn't hurt me,' she said. 'He loves me, why should he hurt me?'

'Well,' Chris said thoughtfully, 'I know he fancies you—he has from the start, but—well, he fancies a lot of women. He never gets too involved, though, not normally. Perhaps he thinks women are only after his money. You do realise that he's quite out of your social sphere, don't you? He and his family are rolling in money. Still, he makes sure he enjoys his status and all the perks it brings him.' She looked down at her glass. 'I suppose it must make you feel quite insecure where women are concerned—all that money. Not that that has ever stopped him having plenty of girl-friends, of course.'

'You don't have to draw me a picture,' Stacy told her sister. 'I'm not so naïve as to think he didn't have anyone else before me.'

Chris buttered herself a roll. 'Well, I just hope you know what you're doing, darling. I shouldn't want to see you end up with nothing.'

Stacy frowned. 'Of course I won't. I'm quite confident that Felipe means what he says. He wouldn't have asked me to marry him if he didn't.'

'But it was very sudden—you must make sure you're not just infatuated.'

'I'm not,' Stacy said, becoming annoyed.

'What are you doing today?' Chris asked, realising a change of subject was necessary.

'We're going to buy my ring this morning. Felipe is taking me to a jewellers in Mahón. He says they have some fabulous rings there and I'll be spoilt for choice.'

'Well, make sure you have the most expensive, darling,' said Chris. 'You might be able to pawn it later if it doesn't work out.'

'Oh, don't be so pessimistic!' Stacy said sternly. 'Of course it will work out—what's the matter with you this morning?'

Chris gave her a weak smile. 'Oh, I must have got out of bed the wrong side,' she replied.

'You should have stayed in bed longer. You didn't have to get up just because I did. I shall only be out for a short while. Felipe has got to work later, but he said he wanted me to have the ring as soon as possible, so that I couldn't forget I belonged to him—as if I would!'

'Well, I can see Daddy's going to be in for a surprise when he gets here,' Chris laughed. 'He lets you loose for two weeks and look what happens!'

Fernando joined them a few minutes later and breakfast was completed with a teasing atmosphere, everyone in good spirits. Felipe picked Stacy up half an hour later and they made their way to Mahón to choose a ring. Felipe looked different in his immaculate business suit of severe black, his white shirt made him look even more tanned than usual. But he still gazed down at Stacy with love in his eyes.

They found a small, exclusive jewellers and Felipe spoke in rapid Spanish to the deferential gentleman behind the counter. He produced many trays of sparkling rings and bade them enter a small room behind the counter where they could choose in peace. Stacy was dazzled by the array set before her.

'Felipe, these must cost a fortune!' she said in a small voice.

He dismissed the statement with a wave of his hand. 'For you, nothing is too expensive. You should be looking for a ring that pleases you, not at the price.'

'Let me see,' she pondered, realising that she had offended him by mentioning the cost, 'how about that—oh yes, that's beautiful.'

The hovering jeweller extracted the ring for Felipe to look at.

'Yes indeed, it is beautiful,' he agreed, holding the ring up to the light. He took Stacy's hand and pushed it on to her finger, looking first at the ring and then at Stacy. 'What do you think, *amada*?'

'Oh, Felipe, it's lovely,' she whispered. The solitaire diamond with its dainty filigree shoulders was indeed beautiful.

'Are you sure you would not like to look at some more before you decide?' Felipe asked.

'No, no, I'm quite happy with this; more than happy, in fact,' she replied, near to tears with emotion.

'Good, then that one it shall be,' said Felipe, lifting her hand and kissing her fingers before removing the ring and giving it to the jeweller.

The little man flapped around him like a mother hen, talking rapidly. Five minutes later they were leaving the shop, after the little jeweller had taken Stacy's hand and shaken it heartily, talking all the time.

'He says I am a lucky man to have met someone as beautiful as you,' Felipe translated, a twinkle in his eyes. 'He says you are *muy hermosa*—very lovely.'

Stacy smiled and said, '*Gracias*,' blushing prettily at the compliments.

Felipe said he had not much time before his meeting and drove rapidly back to Cala Galdaña, but instead of turning left to the villa he turned right.

'Where are we going?' Stacy asked.

'I am taking you to a quiet spot where I can present you with your ring properly,' he told her.

The road opened out into a flat plateau on top of the cliff, leading nowhere. The view was breathtaking, the whole expanse of the bay visible from that height. Felipe got out of the car, and Stacy did the same. They stood looking across the vista before them for a few minutes in silence and then he turned her towards him, the look in his eyes leaving her weak.

'I could curse this meeting, I would much rather have spent the day with you. We could have gone out on the boat together, but it is not to be.' He took the little leather box from his pocket and removed the ring. The sun caught the facets of the diamond and it flashed in a hundred rainbow colours. Felipe took her hand and slowly pushed the ring on to it. Before she had time to look down and admire it he had dragged her against him, his mouth seeking hers in a hungry passion. Stacy wrapped her arms around him, as eager as he for a closer contact.

She felt as if she were drowning in her own emotions, and the trembling of Felipe's body against hers told her that he was feeling the same. Eventually he had to drag himself away.

'I must go. This board meeting is important, if it were not I would stay with you.' He opened the car door and pushed Stacy towards it. 'Come on, in you get. I should have waited until tomorrow to give you your ring, but I couldn't wait. See what you have done to me!'

Stacy smiled at him. 'Good, if you can make me behave out of character I'm glad I can do the same to you.'

'Oh, you have succeeded in doing many things that I have never let any woman do before. You have got under my skin, for a start.'

'Tell me,' Stacy teased.

'No!' he said. 'I do not want you to know all my secrets just yet. A man has to have some pride left.'

'What sort of business do you do, then? You can tell me about that, can't you?'

'Oh yes, I am in the hotel business, *amada*. Luxury hotels for rich holidaymakers who enjoy the creature comforts. We have a profitable *finca* too. But if I do not hurry, I shall be in the doghouse.'

'Where did you learn to speak such good English? I wish I could speak Spanish as well.'

'All these questions—now, when I'm in a hurry! I went to school in England for a time and to university. As for you learning Spanish, I intend to remedy that as soon as possible; I will teach you. Now we must go.'

He let out the clutch and they glided almost silently away. On the return journey he told Stacy that they would be formally engaged when her father arrived for a week's visit on Saturday. They arranged a small dinner party for the family on that day to celebrate and then Felipe hurriedly dropped her off at the villa. He kissed her swiftly on the lips.

'That is all you're getting for now, *querida*, or I shall not want to go,' he told her as he drove away.

'I'll see you tonight,' Stacy shouted after him, and he raised his hand in salute.

Stacy felt guilty. She was sure she would be bored all afternoon without Felipe's company and mentally apologised to her sister for the thought. She was proved wrong, though. Fernando had arranged to take them out to lunch.

'We thought we'd go to Fornells,' he said. 'It's a little fishing village, but it gets its fair share of tourists now as well. I thought it would keep you busy.'

'I should love to go,' Stacy replied. She suddenly remembered her ring and quickly held out her hand, wriggling her fingers so that the diamond sparkled.

'Oh, you've got it already,' Chris commented, coming to look.

'Yes, we couldn't wait. It's too lovely to leave lying in a box. The setting's platinum.'

'It's a beautiful ring,' Fernando told her. 'Do you not think so, Christine?'

'Oh yes, fantastic. Not the sort of thing you'd get out of one of those ten-pence machines at the fair, is it? I see you took my advice—it looks very expensive.'

'I picked it because I liked it—the price had

nothing to do with it. In fact I've no idea how much it cost,' Stacy told her.

Fernando looked at his wife thoughtfully. 'The price of an engagement ring is not what we should concern ourselves with—it is the sentiment behind it that matters.'

'Oh yes, of course it is,' Chris replied, bowing her head.

As they drove off towards Fornells Stacy and Fernando chatted happily; neither of them seemed to notice that Chris was unusually silent. However, she seemed to cheer up after Fernando had asked her if she had a headache, when he realised that she was not joining in the conversation.

It was mid-afternoon when they arrived home. They had eaten in a small restaurant facing the harbour and Fernando had taken them to see the harbour wall, where hundreds of cats had made their homes. There were some shops tucked away in the narrow streets, and he patiently accompanied the girls as they browsed around each one.

They sat around the pool on sun-loungers for most of the afternoon. But it was so hot that Stacy spent quite some time in the swimming pool. Chris joined her on one occasion and they played a halfhearted ball game until they were out of breath. Chezzie kept them well supplied with ice-cold drinks.

At six-thirty Stacy went up to her room to shower and wash her hair and prepare for the evening ahead. She took time over her preparations, making sure she looked her best for Felipe. Chris had unnerved her slightly with her gloomy predictions and she needed to look her best to give herself confidence. Searching through her wardrobe, she eventually decided on a rust-coloured dress which her father had bought for her especially for the holiday. It was made from cool cotton and she decided that on such a hot evening it would be ideal to wear. It was a simple style, shoe-string straps, a high bustline and a flowing skirt. She completed the effect with the shawl which she had bought from Ciudadela on her first day with Felipe. Not too bad, she thought to herself, looking critically into the mirror.

Entering the lounge, Stacy immediately noticed Felipe sitting casually on the sofa, legs sprawled in front of him, talking to Fernando. They both rose as she approached, a custom which Stacy was unused to and which still embarrassed her slightly. Felipe came forward and kissed her cheek, putting his arm around her waist.

'You look delightful, *querida*; good enough to eat,' he told her.

Stacy smiled back at him. 'Thank you.'

'I will agree with you there, Felipe,' said Fernando, passing Stacy her usual glass of sherry.

Chris arrived at that moment and Fernando took her hand, pulling her to his side. 'Ah, now we both are equal,' he said triumphantly to Felipe. 'We both have a beautiful woman to feast our eyes on.'

Chris laughed. 'Flatterer!' she told her husband.

They went in to dinner happily. During the first course the telephone rang and Fernando went to see who it was. He came back about five minutes later.

'Christine, that was your father, but when he heard we were eating he did not want to disturb you. He is coming on Friday instead of Saturday, so he will have more time to recover from the journey before our party. He asked after you, Stacy, he hoped you were enjoying yourself.'

'Oh, Fernando, why didn't you call me?' Chris complained.

'I wanted to,' he countered, 'but Henry would not hear of it, he said you'd see him soon enough.'

'That sounds just like Dad,' Chris said wryly.

'He was quite happy to come on Friday,' Fernando continued. 'I told him we were having a party, but I didn't tell him what it was for. I thought that was best left to you.'

The meal passed off very pleasantly. They left the table replete and retired to the lounge to sink into the soft furniture and listen to some records. Before he left them Felipe took Stacy into the garden to kiss her goodnight. His kisses were passionate, but he kept a tight control on himself and she returned to the house feeling slightly dissatisfied.

CHAPTER THREE

THE next morning Stacy was woken by her sister shaking her.

'Wake up Stacy, wake up!' she called.

'Wh-what's the matter?' Stacy asked, still half asleep.

'Felipe's just phoned. He wants to know if you'd like to fly over to Majorca with him for the day. It's a business trip, actually, but he says that it shouldn't take him more than a couple of hours to clear that up. You could spend the rest of the day sightseeing or something, I suppose. Do you want to go?'

'Oh yes, I want to. How long have I got to get

ready?' Stacy asked, pushing her hair from her eyes and yawning.

'An hour,' Chris replied. 'You've certainly joined the jet-set with a vengeance, haven't you? Jetting off to Majorca for the day!'

'You don't mind do you? I won't go if you don't want me too.'

'Me? Of course I don't mind, darling. You go and enjoy yourself. Fernando says it will do you good to get out and about. Hurry up and get ready.'

'What shall I wear?' Stacy asked, climbing inelegantly out of bed.

'Oh, something cool, I suppose. An uncrushable sun-dress, something like that. You'd better take a bikini too—just in case it gets too hot and you fancy a dip in the sea.'

'Right, I'd better have a shower quickly,' Stacy replied.

'I'll get your breakfast prepared,' said Chris as she left the room.

Within half an hour Stacy was dressed and downstairs eating a light breakfast. She had packed a small vanity case, containing her bikini and a small towel. She had also included a pair of flat sandals, just in case she had to walk any distance. She said goodbye to Fernando and Chris and hurried over to Felipe's villa with minutes to spare.

She rang the doorbell and the housekeeper admitted her with a broad smile. Felipe was in his study, writing rapidly. Stacy lovingly watched the bent dark head and thoughtful expression on his face before saying his name softly to attract his attention. He stood up immediately and came round the desk to greet her.

'*Querida*, you are coming with me?' he asked, kissing her tenderly on the lips before she could reply.

'Yes, of course I am. Did you think I'd refuse?'

Felipe took both her hands in his and kissed them alternately. He was formally dressed this morning in a dark suit, white shirt and neat tie. 'I hoped not. I thought perhaps you might not have had time to prepare yourself, though.'

Stacy laughed. 'I don't take hours to get up, you know. I hardly wear any make-up either, so I don't need to spend all day over that.'

'I know, you are a natural beauty and I love you,' Felipe told her, drawing her into the circle of his arms.

Stacy relaxed against him, resting her head against his broad chest. He raised her chin and kissed her and she clung to him to stop herself from falling.

'I adore you,' he said softly, 'but I must finish my report before we go. Would you like some coffee while you're waiting?'

'No, thanks, I've only just had breakfast. But you carry on, I'll just sit here and wait until you finish.'

'I find it hard to concentrate while you are around,' Felipe admitted.

'Well,' said Stacy, 'you're going to have to get used to me being around, Felipe—you might as well start now.'

'Yes,' he sighed, melodramatically, 'I suppose you are right.'

Stacy sat on the comfortable leather armchair and waited patiently for him to finish. At last he put away his pen and filed the papers in his briefcase.

'My business will not take long, *querida*, then we will have the rest of the day to ourselves.'

'Where are we actually going to?' she asked him.

'To Palma initially, but after that we can go

wherever we please. Is there anywhere you would particularly like to visit?'

Stacy shook her head. 'No, I'm afraid I don't really know anything about the place. I'll leave all that to you.'

'You could look around the shops in Palma if you wish while I conduct my business—as long as you do not get lost or wander away from the main thoroughfares,' Felipe said as he tidied his desk.

'I'll try not to,' she promised teasingly.

Felipe drove to the airport and checked in at reception. 'Come on,' he said, 'we can go across to the aircraft now.'

Stacy followed him across the tarmac and was surprised to end up by a reasonably small aeroplane which had been brought out for them.

'Is this it?' she asked.

'Yes. What is wrong with it?' Felipe asked.

'Nothing, but I thought it would be—well, you know, a proper plane.'

He laughed. 'This is a proper plane, *querida*—it is one of my private jets.'

'*One* of them—how many have you got?' Stacy asked in a surprised tone.

'Three,' Felipe replied. 'It is necessary for the family to be able to get from place to place quickly at times—business depends on it.'

'You don't fly it yourself, do you?' she asked him.

'But of course—you are not afraid of my flying ability, are you?'

'Well, no. But you didn't tell me it was this sort of plane—I thought it would be—you know, like a charter plane, the sort I came from England on.'

'This, my dear child, is a Hawker Siddeley executive jet! I am very proud of it, it is the best plane we have, so do not make fun. Come, you will be most impressed when you see the inside—I hope.'

He helped Stacy up the steps and into the cockpit. A confusion of dials and switches confronted her and she looked up at him in surprise.

'How on earth do you know what's what in here?' she asked.

'Oh, it is quite simple when you have been flying for as long as I have. I have been piloting planes for many years—I achieved my pilot's licence when I was twenty-one.'

'Show-off!' Stacy mocked goodnaturedly.

Felipe opened the door from the cockpit to the cabin and she looked about her with wide eyes. It was just as if she had walked into someone's plush lounge. There were fixed armchairs dotted around the large interior, a thickly carpeted floor, a coffee table in the centre of the room and dainty curtains at the windows.

'You could almost live in this!' she exclaimed in wonder.

'Yes, I suppose you could,' Felipe replied. 'There is even a bathroom through the door over there.' He turned back to the cockpit. 'Do you want to sit with me at the controls?'

'Oh yes, please.'

'Well, we had better get under way, then,' he said.

He seated Stacy beside him and secured her safety belt around her. He donned a pair of headphones and began an involved conversation in Spanish with the control tower. Stacy marvelled at the ease with which he made his check of the aircraft and was so interested in what he was doing that she almost jumped out of her skin when she looked up and found that they were in the air.

It was not like the flight she had arrived on from England at all. Being in the cockpit meant that she could see far more of the scenery, and she watched the runway disappear beneath them quite nervously. When they were at the required height Felipe told her to undo her seat belt if she wished.

'Shall we have some coffee now?' he asked.

'Lovely,' Stacy replied shakily.

'You are not afraid, are you, *querida*?' Felipe asked, noticing her pallor.

'Er—not really. My stomach turned over when we left the ground, that's all.'

He stood up and walked out of the cockpit, leaving Stacy still sitting in her seat.

'Felipe!' she cried in panic, running out after him.

'What is wrong?' he asked.

'You—You're not flying the plane—we'll crash!'

He laughed and hugged her tightly.

'Have you never heard of an automatic pilot? I have switched over to that. It is quite safe to leave the controls for a few minutes.'

Stacy was relieved and relaxed against him. 'I've heard of something like that on boats, but I didn't realise aeroplanes had them too.'

'Here, take one of these,' said Felipe, pouring her a steaming cup of coffee. 'We will be there soon, it is only a short flight.'

She fastened her safety belt again when they returned to the cockpit and watched in fascination as they circled the island of Majorca before landing. The wide blue bay of Palma looked like a picture from a holiday brochure. The sea foamed in white waves on to the curved beach and yachts were dotted around on the calm surface of the water.

'Oh, Felipe—look! Isn't it beautiful?'

'Beautiful, certainly. We have picked an excellent day for flying,' he agreed.

They landed some five minutes later and after some formalities they were cleared through Customs and stepped out into the brilliant sunshine again. A car was waiting to take Felipe to his appointment, but he ushered Stacy into it too.

'Would you like to wait for me and read a magazine? Or would you like to look around the shops? It is nine-thirty now—they will all be open.'

'I think I'll look round the shops—the time will pass more quickly then.'

'Very well, I will drop you in the Plaza Mayor— the main square. You must promise me not to wander away from the main streets.'

'I won't get lost,' Stacy laughed.

'You had better not,' Felipe replied. 'I could not bear to lose you.' He put his arms around her and kissed her lips gently—in full view of the driver. Stacy was embarrassed, but Felipe did not seem to care.

'Have you enough money?' he asked softly.

'Yes, plenty,' Stacy told him. 'No one's allowed me to spend any of my own yet!'

Felipe gave his instructions to the driver and they moved out into the steady stream of traffic from the airport. He opened the door for her when they reached the square and kissed her before she climbed out.

'There are many shops in this area,' he told her. 'You should not be bored.'

'I'll be fine—you go and get your business over with. Where shall I meet you?'

'Here—I will be back at eleven-thirty to collect you. Do not be late.'

'I won't,' Stacy assured him, pleased that he should be so concerned about her.

The sun was hot and she decided first to look around the Cathedral. It was not easy to find and she had to wind her way through narrow back streets—against Felipe's wishes—to get there. The interior was cool and dim and Stacy wandered around slowly. There were a few other tourists doing the same and she waited until she saw a couple leave and followed them, hoping they would head back to the main shopping area. She was lucky and they guided her unknowingly back to the square where she had started. She was surprised to see some well known stores in evidence and walked around each one, quite intrigued to find familiar products with foreign wrappings.

At a tiny boutique she stopped to admire the colourful array of clothes on show there, and her eye was immediately caught by a white cheesecloth dress. A full, pleated skirt fell from the lacy bodice and it had dainty shoe-string straps. Stacy decided to try it on and walked boldly into the dimly lit shop. She gestured to the smiling girl behind the counter and was shown a tiny changing room where she was just able to remove her own dress and try the other one on. The shop assistant clapped her hands together and told Stacy she looked '*Muy hermosa*'— very beautiful—and Stacy understood the phrase as it was one which Felipe used quite often to her.

'*Gracias,*' she responded.

She was herself delighted with the dress. She had tanned to a deep golden brown now and the white cheesecloth showed it off perfectly. She went to change back into her sun-dress again and came out of the boutique feeling very pleased with herself.

There was only a quarter of an hour now before Felipe was to collect her, and she decided to sit outside one of the many cafes to wait for him. She raised her face to the sun and closed her eyes against its brilliance.

'*Ola, señorita,*' said a strange voice above her, and Stacy opened her eyes and blinked up at the tall dark stranger hovering near her chair. His eyes ran over her from head to foot and she could feel herself blushing at his scrutiny. She turned away, ignoring the invitation in his eyes, and looked for Felipe's car.

'*Tu eres Alemaña?*' he persisted.

'I don't understand you,' Stacy said coldly.

He was carrying a small briefcase and was obviously on his way to some business appointment—or just coming from one. '*Inglesa!*' he realised. 'Please to sit with you?'

'No,' Stacy replied. 'I'm waiting for my fiancé.'

'He is not here. Me, I am here with you. You like a drink?'

'No.'

He sat down at the table beside her anyway and Stacy immediately stood up, collecting her parcels and walking away. She had never had to deal with such persistency before and was not at all sure how to handle it.

'You not like me?' the Spaniard continued.

'Go away!' Stacy replied angrily.

'You lovely lady. I like.'

'Well, I don't like you. *Go away!*'

Suddenly she recognised Felipe, pulling up in a small sports car some yards away, and rushed over to him.

'Oh, I'm so glad to see you!' she told him, sliding

in beside him and wrapping her arms around his neck.

'What is the matter, *querida*? What has happened?'

'Oh, some man tried to pick me up—but I'm all right, really.'

'I knew I should not have let you out on your own. I knew something would happen.'

'Nothing's happened—I've only been waiting for two minutes at the most, there wasn't time for anything to happen.'

'You should have come with me and waited—it would have been safer.'

'Felipe, I can't live in a glass case! You can't protect me against everybody all the time, and I don't want to end up never going out just in case someone speaks to me.'

Felipe sighed. 'You are right, of course.'

'I went round the Cathedral,' she said to change the subject. 'I followed some other tourists, so I didn't have to find my own way. It was lovely and cool inside. Then I followed some others back into the square again and looked around the shops. I didn't know there was a Woolworths here! It seemed really funny seeing it in the middle of all those little Spanish shops. I went in and looked round.'

'You made good use of your time, *querida*.'

'Oh yes, I took some photographs of those donkey carts too. The donkeys had hats on with holes cut out for their ears—they looked really sweet.'

Felipe smiled and squeezed her hand, his anger forgotten.

'It is like seeing everything again for the first time, when I am with you, as I have said before.' He put the car into gear and pulled smoothly away. 'I am

going to take you across the island to Puerto Pollensa for lunch. I think you will like it there—it is
not quite so commercialised as this side. It will not
take long to get there—we will be in time for
lunch.'

'Sounds great. Where did you get this car from,
by the way?' Stacy asked, waving her hand around.
'It's very smart.'

'It belongs to someone at the office in Palma, and
I borrowed it for today.

It is easier to manoeuvre than my own. We can
take it back before we leave and the chauffeur will
take us back to the airport.'

Stacy lay back in her seat and relaxed. She
thought of her own mode of transport at home—a
double-decker bus. Life had certainly changed dra-
matically since she had left England. She had not
asked Felipe where they would live, but presumed
that his villa in Menorca was his normal base. It did
not occur to her that she might miss England, although her father would be so far away she was quite
happy to uproot herself and live anywhere as long as
Felipe was with her. That he lived in such a beautiful island anyway was an added bonus.

'What are you thinking about, *querida*?' he
asked.

'I was thinking how lucky I am,' she replied
honestly.

'Lucky?'

'Yes, to have you and for being able to enjoy living
here in the sun. I didn't realise why Chris didn't
want to come home at first—I thought she was a
fool to want to live with a load of foreigners—but it
was I who was the fool.'

'If you are lucky,' said Felipe, 'then I am doubly

lucky to have been in the right place at the right time to meet you.'

As they drove across the island Stacy noticed many watermills turning lazily in the soft breeze.

'What are they for?' she asked.

'To irrigate the land,' Felipe explained. 'It is very dry in the middle of the island and the farmers use the watermills to pump lifegiving water to their peanut plants.'

'Peanuts?' she queried.

'Yes, as far as you can see, on both sides of the road there are peanut plants.'

They reached Pollensa just after twelve o'clock and walked slowly along the road adjacent to the harbour. There was a long stretch of pale golden sand bordered by palm trees, and Stacy itched to dive into the deep blue water to cool off. Felipe stopped at a waterside restaurant for lunch and they sat outside under an enormous striped umbrella. Their meal was delicious. Felipe recommended a liqueur ice cream to finish with and Stacy almost choked as the Cointreau she had chosen took her breath away.

'I shall be drunk on this,' she laughed. 'It's absolutely swimming in Cointreau! I thought you'd only get about a spoonful. Taste it.'

She held up a spoonful and Felipe opened his mouth to receive it. He raised his dark eyebrows. '*Dios*, you are right! You will have to have a black coffee after that to sober up again.'

'I don't know—I rather fancy the idea of getting drunk on ice cream—but no one would ever believe me.' She looked out longingly across the water. 'Can we have a swim later? I brought my bikini with me and that water looks lovely.'

'Yes, of course you can, but only after your lunch has gone down.'

'Right. Would you like to see the dress I bought?' She held out the packet and Felipe took it and peered inside. He lifted out the dress and held it up.

'Very nice. You will look delightful in it, *querida*,' he said, his eyes shining.

'Oh, I do,' Stacy laughed. 'The assistant said I was *muy hermosa*.'

They walked around the many antique and gift shops along the harbour and Felipe insisted on buying her a beautiful enamelled necklace which she had much admired in a shop. It had been made locally and Stacy knew that she would always remember the happy day she had spent on Majorca whenever she wore it. The fact that Felipe had bought it for her made it extra special.

'It will look good with your new dress,' he told her.

'I know, I'd already thought of that,' Stacy agreed.

A couple of hours later they sat on a tiny, secluded beach. Stacy couldn't wait to get into the water and dashed off to get changed into her bikini. As she expected, the water felt cold after the heat of the sun, but after the initial shock she swam around freely. Felipe did not join her but he watched her every move from his position on the beach.

She came up out of the water some time later and blushed as he watched her progress up the beach. He reached up and took her hand as she got closer and pulled her down beside him. He had taken off his tie and undone his shirt, and Stacy looked at him lovingly. His strong, bronzed features were so familiar to her now, but she knew that when she was away from him it was always difficult to remember every detail of his face correctly.

'Mmmm,' he said, 'you look—how do you say—good enough to eat?'

'Thank you,' she replied happily.

When he kissed her she wrapped her salty arms around his neck and pressed close. The feel of her almost naked body sent wild sensations through him which he found difficult to control. He pressed Stacy back on to the hot sand and continued to kiss her feverishly.

'Your suit!' she protested.

'Is of no matter,' he told her, returning his lips to hers.

Stacy didn't notice the discomfort of the hot sand and clung to him, revelling in the strength and possession of his lips. He feathered light kisses across her eyelids and caressed the soft skin of her midriff.

'I love you desperately,' he whispered, 'and I want you desperately too. Tell me that you love me.'

'I love you, Felipe,' she responded. 'I love you very much.'

His lips returned to hers, exploring her sensitive mouth in an agony of passion. Eventually, when he could stand the strain no longer, he pushed himself away from her.

'Stacy, you are driving me crazy. I am a fool to be alone with you like this. You go to my head far too quickly, and I do not want to hurt you.'

Stacy didn't move—it was impossible. Her limbs felt like jelly and her blood was still pounding wildly through her veins, making her feel quite dizzy.

'Stacy?' Felipe queried in a worried tone when she didn't move.

'You haven't hurt me, Felipe,' she said huskily,

raising herself up on one elbow. Felipe's expression was pained and she realised that it had been hard for him to pull away when he had.

'Look at that boat with the red sails,' she said, trying to ease the situation. 'Right out there on the horizon. It looks like a toy.'

'We will be able to go anywhere we want on the *Gaviota* when we are married,' Felipe mused. 'We can cruise around the Greek Islands and moor in some deserted spot and no one will ever find us.'

'What would happen to your business then—and your family?' Stacy asked.

'My business seems of little importance since I have met you.'

'What's your mother like, Felipe?' she asked suddenly.

'My mother? Well, she is like any other mother, I suppose. Of course, I love her dearly. She is a great help to me in the running of the *finca*. She rules with an iron hand, but she is a kindhearted person. She speaks very highly of me too,' he added mischievously.

'Do you think she will approve of me?' Stacy asked quietly.

'But of course! She will be glad that I have at last found someone I wish to spend my life with. I think she had given up hope almost of me ever finding someone suitable.'

'You must have had many girl-friends,' Stacy remarked miserably.

Felipe looked at her, his heart in his eyes. Her blue eyes looked enormous in the small face and her fair hair had been bleached pale gold by the sun. She looked a picture of youthful beauty and health and he ran his hand lovingly down the side of her face.

'None of them as beautiful as you, *querida*,' was his only reply.

Stacy turned her head and kissed his stroking palm before lying down on the sand to dry in the heat of the sun.

They returned to Palma via the mountains in the north of the island. The roads were steep and winding and Stacy held her breath as Felipe negotiated them carefully.

'It's almost as bad as flying,' she said, 'but the view's spectacular, I must admit. Just look at those beautiful trees growing right up there with hardly any soil to live on. Oh—perhaps you'd better not,' she laughed. 'I'd rather you kept your eyes on the road.'

'I am afraid I shall have to,' Felipe replied. 'Although I could think of other things I would prefer to look at.'

'Like what?'

'Like you, of course, need you ask?'

Stacy was overjoyed to see oranges and lemons growing on trees by the roadsides. Felipe stopped at a small shack right up in the mountains where they picked oranges from the trees and pressed them immediately to make cool, refreshing juice. Stacy tried some and was surprised to find how cold it was. She also bought a fresh, juicy fig, almost the size of a pear, to take back for her father. He was due to arrive at the end of the week for his holiday and she was sure he would never have tasted one before.

They drove slowly back to Palma where they changed cars and Felipe's chauffeur took them back to the airport. It looked different at night—a mass of different coloured lights which Felipe explained the meanings of as they crossed to their small aircraft. Stacy sat in the cockpit with him again and was not so frightened of the take-off this time. It was dark and she wasn't so aware of the distance between themselves and the ground. The lights of Majorca twinkling far below were a fascination to her. She watched the lights of cars winding around the roads and could see lights from the boats moored in the harbour reflecting off the dark water. The Cathedral at Palma could be seen plainly, spotlights lighting up the pleasing architecture brilliantly.

'It's like Fairyland,' she told Felipe.

She held her breath as they touched down on the tarmac, but Felipe made a smooth landing and they were soon through Customs and out into the cool night air. Felipe drove home slowly and by the time they reached the villa Stacy was pleasantly tired.

'It was a lovely day, Felipe, I really enjoyed it. Chris said I'd joined the jet-set with a vengeance— flying off to Majorca for the day.'

'She sounds envious of you,' Felipe mused.

'Oh no, Chris isn't like that, I think she was just pleased,' Stacy assured him innocently.

He pulled up outside the villa and switched off the engine.

'Talking about jetting around—I have to go home tomorrow. I have the unpleasant duty of sacking one of my foremen who has been engaged in some illicit trading. We are very close to Tangiers, across the water, and he has been selling our produce to a trader over there. It is hard to find good men. The labourers in the fields are excellent, but the more intelligent they get and the higher the position they attain, the less respect they seem to have for their employers. It is very bad.'

'When will you be back?' Stacy asked.

'Oh, by Friday, definitely. I have a few other things to attend to while I am there. But do not worry, I shall be here in time for our engagement party on Saturday—nothing would stop me from getting back for that.'

'Good,' Stacy replied, feeling a little miserable to think that she wouldn't see him for a couple of days.

'You will think about me while I am gone?' he asked, drawing her closer.

'All the time,' she told him.

'I will ring you when I get home, to tell you that I arrived safely and to see how you are. Would you like that?'

'Oh yes, please. That'll make the days pass more quickly.'

Felipe smiled and ran a light kiss across her forehead.

'You are such a child, *querida*, in some ways. All the time I fear I shall lose you.'

'No!' Stacy retorted. 'You'll never lose me, I want to be with you.'

'Prove it,' he muttered close to her mouth. 'Kiss me.'

She was still shy of making the first move where he was concerned, but determinedly pressed her lips to his and pulled him closer. His hands fastened around her back and stroked the soft skin, sending wild shivers of pleasure through her body. He pressed her against the seat and half lay across her in the confined space of the car, feverishly kissing her parted lips and holding her so tightly that it hurt. Stacy clung to him blindly, quite happy to be carried away on the tide of emotion which engulfed them, not realising where it might lead.

Chris was in the kitchen talking to Chezzie when Stacy walked into the villa.

'Ah, you're back, then?' she said unnecessarily. 'Had a good day?'

'Marvellous! Felipe pilots his own plane, you know. He's very good. You should see the inside of it—it's just like your lounge. Thick carpet, arm-chairs—the lot! I couldn't believe it.'

'I'm sure you couldn't,' Chris replied offhandedly. 'I hope you're not going to get hurt.'

'What do you mean?' asked Stacy.

'Well,' Chris replied, shrugging her slim shoulders, 'you should know that people who have everything get tired of things very quickly. You should have more sense than to get so involved.'

'But that's ridiculous! We're getting engaged, Felipe and I—of course I'm involved.'

'Well, I just hope it all works out for you, darling,' Chris replied, walking from the kitchen and into the lounge.

'Why shouldn't it?' Stacy persisted, following her. 'Felipe loves me and I love him—what's wrong with that?'

'Are you sure it's him you love,' her sister replied, 'or his fancy plane and his expensive sports car?'

'That's a horrible thing to say! I'd love Felipe if he had nothing!'

'Then you're a bigger fool than I thought you were,' Chris replied.

At that moment Fernando walked in and Chris immediately became bubbly and charming.

'Oh, there you are, darling. Shall we have a drink

before we go to bed? What would you like, Stacy—sherry?—Martini?'

'I—I'll have a sweet sherry, please,' Stacy mumbled.

'Have you had a good time, Stacy?' Fernando asked.

'Lovely, thank you,' she replied.

'Well, tell us where you went and what you did, then,' Chris joined in.

'We went to Palma first because Felipe had an appointment there. I walked around the shops and went to the Cathedral while he was away. Then he drove me to Puerto Pollensa for lunch. It was really nice there, and after we'd looked around the shops I went for a swim in the sea. We drove back through the mountains and I had some fresh orange juice straight from the tree.'

Fernando laughed.

'Really,' Stacy continued. 'They pick the oranges and press them straight away. I bought a fresh fig for Daddy, I don't suppose he'll have had one before. I bought myself a dress too, in Palma. Do you want to look?'

'But of course we do,' Fernando assured her.

Stacy ran back to the kitchen and picked up her parcel.

'Look, this is it—do you like it?' she asked.

'Very nice,' Chris admitted.

'I think you will look delightful in it,' Fernando told her.

She then showed them the brightly coloured enamelled necklace which Felipe had bought. Fernando admired it and Chris agreed that it would go well with her dress.

The next day dragged, but Stacy refused to move far from the house in case she missed Felipe's call. It

came at twelve-thirty, just as she was about to go in
to lunch. He told her that he had arrived quite safely
and he wished he could have taken her with him,
but there was far too much business to see to and he
would not have had time to look after her. They
spoke for almost half an hour and by the time Stacy
went in to lunch, hers was almost cold.

'I don't mind,' she said happily; it was worth a
cold dinner to speak to Felipe.

Fernando offered to take Chris and herself out for
the afternoon and they both agreed that it would be
nice. He took them to Son Bou, which sported the
largest beach on Menorca. To get to the beach they
had to pass through a tunnel carved out of solid rock
which Stacy insisted on taking a picture of. They
walked around the ruins of a basilica dating back to
the fourth or fifth century and then lay contentedly
on the beach all afternoon. By five o'clock they had
had enough and Fernando drove them to a quiet
restaurant in Mahón for dinner.

Only one day to go, Stacy thought when they
returned home and she prepared for bed. Only one
day and then Felipe would come back.

CHAPTER FOUR

SATURDAY dawned as bright and clear as all the previous days, but it was special. Stacy leapt out of bed,
unable to contain her excitement. Today she would
be officially engaged. The night before she, Chris
and Fernando had gone across to the airport to collect her father. They had watched excitedly as he

came down the steps of the aircraft and had run to meet him when he passed through passport control.

Mr Barker had hugged his children fondly and shaken Fernando's hand.

'Oh, it's good to see you, Dad,' Chris had said, almost in tears.

'It's good to see you too, love,' Mr Barker told her. 'That husband of yours seems to be looking after you—you look well enough.'

'I am. And you don't look too bad yourself. Did you enjoy the flight?'

'Not too bad, I suppose. It was better than the plane I travelled on during the war—that's for certain.' He turned to Stacy. 'And what about you? Enjoying yourself, are you? You've got a lovely tan.'

'Fabulous, Dad, it's really lovely here.' She did not mention Felipe, it was not the time and place to discuss such things.

They had driven back across the island to the villa and Mr Barker had been a little bemused by his surroundings at first.

'Well,' he had said, looking about him, 'It's a bit different from Birmingham, but I suppose you get used to it in time.'

Both girls had laughed.

'Oh, Dad,' said Chris, 'trust you to say something like that!'

The villa itself had confounded him even more. He had walked around with Fernando and the girls shaking his head and muttering, 'Well, I never!'

Stacy drew him to one side back in the *sala* and told him about Felipe.

'Oh no, you can't do a thing like that,' he had protested. 'It's so sudden—you can't have known him five minutes.'

'I feel as though I've known him all my life, Dad,' Stacy said honestly. 'I can't imagine life without him now. We just fit well together; the fact that we've only known each other a short time doesn't seem to matter.'

'I can't believe it,' muttered Henry, sitting down on the nearest chair. 'It doesn't seem five minutes since you were a baby.'

'I'm not a baby any more, though, Dad. I didn't think I'd ever be so sure of anything—but about Felipe I'm absolutely certain. He's great, Dad, I know you'll like him a lot when you meet him.'

Mr Barker took her hands and sighed. 'Well, love, you're old enough to know your own mind, I suppose, and if you're certain he's the one for you I wish you every happiness.'

Stacy had kissed him and hugged his sagging shoulders. 'Thanks, Dad,' she said.

'These damn foreigners,' he had said laughingly. 'Both my girls snatched from under my nose as soon as my back's turned. Always said you couldn't trust foreigners!'

Fernando had joined in the laughter, not taking the least offence at his remarks. 'Let us have a drink to celebrate the good news,' he said. 'What would you like, Henry?'

'I'll have a brandy, please—double. I think I deserve it, don't you?'

'Certainly,' Fernando replied, pouring out a large measure.

And now it was Saturday. Stacy went to take a shower and then dressed in a pair of jeans and a sleeveless tee-shirt. She combed her hair thoroughly but did not bother with any make-up before going downstairs. Chris was up already and so was

Fernando, but Mr Barker had not yet come down.

'He must be tired, poor lamb,' said Chris when Stacy remarked on his absence. 'He isn't getting any younger, you know, and I suppose the flight was a bit of a strain. I suppose your news gave him a bit of a shock as well. He hadn't anticipated that.'

'Neither had I when I arrived,' Stacy replied, 'but I think he'll be happy when he meets Felipe. He'll know I've picked the right person.'

'Yes,' Chris replied, 'I'm sure he'll be overjoyed. Do you want some grapefruit juice?'

'Please.'

'I heard you are going to spend some money today,' Fernando said to Stacy. 'Do not encourage Christine to buy the most expensive outfit—anyone would think she was getting engaged herself again! She has a wardrobe full of clothes, but she insists on having something new for tonight—women!'

'I'll try,' Stacy laughed. 'I'll look at the price tag first and tell her it doesn't suit her if it costs too much—mind you, I don't suppose she'll believe me.'

'Are you all set for the big day?' Chris asked. 'Except for a new dress, of course—no second thoughts, I hope?'

'None at all,' Stacy replied.

'I hope Felipe feels the same,' Chris said quietly.

'Of course he does,' Stacy told her. 'Why shouldn't he?'

Chris shook her head and smiled wistfully. 'No reason, I suppose.'

Stacy turned away, annoyed. 'What time are we going to Mahón?'

'We'll start out straight after breakfast. I expect Dad will want a lie-in, but Fernando will be home to look after him anyway. We shouldn't be all that long. I know a fantastic dress shop in Mahón, I'm sure they'll be able to fix you up with something befitting the occasion.'

'Good,' said Stacy, munching on a piece of toast.

They started out half an hour later, both girls enjoying the prospect of buying new clothes. At the shop they browsed through a multitude of long and short dresses and Chris eventually decided on a long cream creation, Grecian style, which showed her red hair and good figure off to perfection.

Stacy chose a sleek short black dress with cap sleeves and a close-fitting waist. The back of the dress was cut very low, almost to the waist in a vee shape and the straight skirt was split from above the knee. A spray of sparkling beads arranged flower-like spread over one breast and Stacy twirled in front of the mirror, watching them sparkle.

'That's very nice,' Chris told her. 'I'm sure Felipe will be most impressed.'

Stacy pirouetted in front of the mirror again. 'Oh yes, I'll take this one.'

They bought shoes and handbags to go with their dresses and left the shop loaded down with parcels.

'Come on,' said Chris, 'I think we deserve a drink, don't you?'

They chose one of the cafés in the main square and sat outside in the sunshine. Before returning to Cala Galdaña they looked around a few more shops and Stacy bought herself a diamond clip for her hair and some new make-up. They were back at the villa in time for lunch. After a crisp salad and cold chicken they all retired for a siesta to conserve their energies for the coming dinner party.

Felipe phoned Stacy just before she went to her room.

'Stacy, *querida*, are you all right?' he asked in a low voice.

'Of course I am,' she replied breezily. 'I've never felt better.'

'*Muy bien*, I just wanted to tell you that I love you and I can't wait to see you tonight. I have missed you all day.'

'It's only three o'clock,' Stacy replied, 'but I know what you mean.'

'I love you,' Felipe repeated.

She realised that he was waiting for her to reciprocate and she did so willingly. 'And I love you too, Felipe, more than I can say.'

She heard his sigh down the earpiece.

'That is good. I wanted to come over this morning and see you before you went shopping, but I had a phone call and was delayed. You had gone when I arrived. I have met your father. I like him; but he subjected me to something bordering on the Inquisition. He is very fond of you.'

'Yes,' Stacy answered, 'I know. He's a lovely old stick, Felipe, Chris and I think the world of him.'

'That is how it should be. I suppose I will have to go now,' he sighed. 'But tonight is ours—I shall not leave your side all evening. I only wish I did not have to leave your side all night either,' he finished huskily.

'I wish that too, Felipe,' Stacy told him truthfully.

'Mmmmm, I think we had better change the subject, don't you? I shall count the minutes until I see you.'

Stacy whispered a few words of endearment and replaced the receiver.

She did not expect to be able to sleep, but within

ten minutes of lying on the top of her bed she was drifting into oblivion.

They were all ready by eight o'clock. Mr Barker had held a clean white handkerchief to the corners of his eyes as Stacy and Chris walked into the lounge where he and Fernando were waiting.

'Your mother would be so proud to see you both,' he mumbled. 'I only wish she was here to see what you've both grown into—beautiful!'

Chris put an arm around his shoulders and hugged him. 'Come on, Dad, don't get upset. I'm sure Mum is keeping an eye on us somehow.'

Fernando turned to Stacy and held out his hands. 'Well, Stacy, I do not recognise you, you look as though you have just walked out of one of those glossy magazines which Christine spends a fortune on. Felipe is a lucky man.'

'Thank you,' Stacy replied, bowing her head in acknowledgement of the compliment.

They walked through the garden and into Felipe's. Mr Barker stared in wonder at the landscaped gardens and beautifully tended lawns.

'I didn't think they had green grass over here,' he said, scratching his head. 'I thought it was all dried up with the sun.'

Chris laughed. 'Normally it would be, Dad, but Felipe can afford to pay a couple of gardeners to keep it looking good. It's surprising what money can do.'

'Well,' her father replied, 'it's put to a good use if it can make a desert into an oasis.'

Chris shrugged. 'Yes, I suppose so,' she had to agree.

Felipe was waiting at the door for them. He looked disturbingly handsome in a beige suit which

accentuated the length of his legs and his broad
shoulders and made his skin look very bronzed
indeed. He put an arm around Stacy and squeezed
her, and her heart turned over as he looked down
into her bright eyes, his own almost black.

'Stacy, I cannot find words—you look—beautiful,
very, very beautiful.' He bent to kiss her lips as the
others walked on into the villa and Stacy could feel
him trembling against her. They followed shortly
afterwards, their arms around each other, and
Felipe invited them into the *sala* for a pre-dinner
drink.

Mr Barker turned to Felipe some moments later.
'Well, son,' he said, 'you've certainly done well for
yourself. How did you manage it? What do you do
for a living?'

'Dad!' Stacy protested, but Felipe laughed!

'I have an estate in Andalusia,' he told them.
'And my family own some luxury hotels. I have
two brothers who run the estate in my absence.
They are younger than I, but very hardworking. I
am the head of the family since my father died ten
years ago. We also have many vineyards in the
vegas—that is the coastal plain of Andalusia. The
rivers flow from the mountains and make the land
very fertile in places. Our vineyards yield excellent
crops of grapes—we make wine for export. You
must all come and see for yourselves.'

'It sounds wonderful,' Stacy said dreamily.

'Oh, it is,' Felipe agreed, looking deeply into her
eyes. 'I cannot wait to take you there and introduce
you to my family—after we are married. You could
all come over for Christmas—that would be good—
yes?'

'That's very good of you, lad—I'm sure we'd all

have a grand time. You do have a proper Christmas, I suppose?'

'Oh yes,' Felipe replied, a smile playing around his lips. 'I promise you we will have a traditional English Christmas in your honour.'

They celebrated with a champagne toast at the dinner table. The meal was delicious—Felipe's housekeeper had excelled herself. Even Mr Barker enjoyed his food. He was most surprised and admitted the fact to the rest of his family.

'Well,' he told them, 'I'm thoroughly enjoying this. I thought we'd be eating all sorts of foreign stuff, but this is delicious. I must admit I'm surprised.'

'I will tell Maria, my cook, that you approve,' Felipe promised, laughing. 'She will be most pleased.'

When they had finished eating they returned to the lounge, and there, on the comfortable sofas, they sat talking and drinking Felipe's own excellent wine until the early hours. Eventually Mr Barker said he had had enough and stood up to leave. He thanked Felipe in his down-to-earth manner for the enjoyable evening and told him he had better look after Stacy or he'd be in trouble. Although the rest of his family laughed Felipe told him quite seriously that he intended to do just that. Fernando and Chris went back to the villa with Mr Barker and Felipe and Stacy walked very slowly behind them.

'I will escort you back,' Felipe told her, bowing over her hand and kissing it politely. But the fire in his dark eyes was anything but tame.

When they reached the bushes which separated the two gardens he turned and took Stacy in his arms.

'*Querida*, I have been waiting to get you to myself

all evening. I like your family very much, but all I could think of was being alone with you.' He bent his head and pressed a gentle kiss on to her lips. 'You look wonderful, especially in that dress. Did you buy it today?'

'Yes,' she replied huskily. 'Chris took me to Mahón, as you know, I bought it there. I'm glad you approve.'

'Approve is far too tame a word,' he laughed softly. 'I should never let you wear that if I were not with you—it does strange things to a man.'

'Mmmm, interesting—tell me?' Stacy teased.

'No, I have to have some secrets; keep my self-respect. I am not used to being brought to my knees by a woman—it is usually the other way around,' he said.

'Arrogant swine!' Stacy exclaimed, and Felipe laughed, hauling her closer to him. She put her arms around his waist and stood closer still. He kissed her deeply, exploring her sensitive mouth with increasing passion. His hands pressed her hips to him and he groaned as she moved against him.

'Stacy, marry me tomorrow, I can't wait any longer—you are like a drug and I am addicted. I cannot get enough of you, not like this.' His hands caressed her back and hips slowly, moving forward until he cupped her breasts. Stacy could not speak, her breath caught in her throat and she felt that her heart would burst with pleasure.

'Felipe,' she cried at last, 'I'll do anything you say—I love you!'

His kiss was so savage it hurt, but she didn't mind a bit.

'Stacy, we will get married in England. I will get a special licence and we can be married by the end of the week. Say you will—I know it does not give you much time, but I do not think you want to wait either.'

'I don't, I don't. Felipe, you don't have to wait at all—I don't mind.'

'Oh, Stacy,' he groaned, his chin resting on the top of her head, 'you do not understand. Do you think I want to make love to you and then immediately return you to your family? Oh no, once I have you in my bed I shall expect you to stay there until I am ready to let you go. I don't think you will have any complaints. I cannot just take satisfaction from you and send you off home. It would be no satisfaction at all to part with you. It would not work. As I said before, you are like a drug—once I have tasted you I will keep coming back for more.'

He kissed her feverishly again and then turned and took her hand. She was still bemused and followed on shaking legs.

'I will speak to your father tomorrow,' Felipe said quietly as they reached the door. He traced a long finger down the side of her face and she trembled at his touch.

'What about your family, Felipe?' she asked. 'Shouldn't you let them know?'

'Of course I will let them know,' he replied smoothly, 'but I am a big boy now, I make my own life. If I let them know immediately they will insist on us flying over to the mainland for them to see you, and then we would have to visit all my relatives—aunts, uncles, cousins and goodness knows who else, and it would be months before we could make our arrangements. My mother would insist on a wildly flamboyant affair with hundreds of guests and speeches which you wouldn't understand, and I

don't think we need all that, Stacy. I know I would
be quite happy if there were to be only us two at our
wedding—if that were possible. No, I prefer to do it
my way, as I always have—they understand that. I
know they will love you when they see you, even if
they are disappointed about not being able to
arrange the wedding.'

He kissed her once more to stop any more questions, and Stacy immediately forgot everything but
the demanding pressure of his mouth and hands.

They spent Sunday on the boat. Mr Barker was
rather dubious about this adventure, but gentle per-
suasion made him agree to accompany them. When
he realised that it wasn't a dinghy he was quite
happy to get on board.

'Will you take us down into Port Mahón again?'
Stacy begged Felipe. 'I'd like you to show Dad
where Nelson was supposed to live and the fortress
of San Felipe. He'd be really interested.'

'Very well, *querida*, we will go to Mahón. I think
one of our ships is in port at the moment. Would
you like to see her?'

'Oh yes. I didn't know you owned a ship as well.'

Felipe laughed. 'Quite a few, to be honest. It is
necessary to keep things in the family if we are to
make a profit. We ship our own wines around the
world, and a few other things as well.'

'Like what?' Stacy asked.

'Oh, various products made from them—olive oil,
carvings made from olive wood, all sorts of things.
We are very self-sufficient.'

'Oh, Felipe,' Stacy said shakily, 'I feel scared. You
have so much and I have so little. We're worlds
apart.'

Felipe put his finger firmly to her lips. 'You bring me yourself, that is all I want from you,' he told her, pressing a gentle kiss to her lips where his finger had previously been. 'We are not worlds apart at all, we were made for each other,' he said. 'Now, let us get under way. The others will be getting impatient.'

They sailed into Mahón and Felipe gave a running commentary as they passed through the islands and into Port Mahón itself. They visited the ship belonging to the Cuevas line and Stacy walked around with Felipe, quite entranced by the deference which the crew showed to them. The captain showed them over the bridge before they disembarked and wished them much happiness in their life together. They boarded the yacht again after a substantial meal at the Yacht Club and cruised slowly around the rocky coastline. Mr Barker decided to try out Felipe's fishing rod, and this kept him occupied for most of the afternoon.

They arrived back at the villa in time for dinner, but Felipe decided to take Stacy out to eat. They went to a small restaurant on the road from Cala Galdaña to Ferrerias—the nearest large village. From the outside it looked like a cowshed, but Felipe parked the car and they walked around the side of the building and into a forecourt which was decidedly Moorish in design—white arches covered with bougainvillea, pots of flowers scattered everywhere—it certainly didn't look like a cowshed now! There was a charcoal grill in one corner and the smell of cooking meat was delicious.

Felipe ordered the meal for both of them and Stacy was not disappointed in his choice. They had succulent steak with an enormous bowl of salad followed by a sweet which comprised ice cream,

Curaçao peaches, pineapple and topped with cream. Felipe told Stacy that it was the house speciality. They washed it all down with an excellent wine and she felt so full that she could hardly breathe.

When Felipe took Stacy back to the villa it was quite late. He kissed her passionately before he left her at the door.

'I have a business appointment tomorrow morning, *querida*,' he said, 'but I will see you in the afternoon—yes?'

'Oh yes, Felipe, of course,' she agreed.

By two o'clock the following day she had not seen Felipe, and she wandered around feeling restless. She decided to walk through the gardens and see if he had arrived back. She noticed his car at the front of the house and a small, racy sports car by its side. As she was about to turn away the door opened and Felipe emerged, preceded by a dark-haired woman who turned and smiled up at him in such a way that Stacy could feel her hackles rise. She turned away, not wanting to see any more, but Felipe had seen her and called to her before she could get away.

'Stacy, I was coming to see you now. I intended to do so before, but as you can see I had a visitor. This is an old acquaintance of mine—Luisa Aquilar—Luisa, this is Stacy Barker.'

The older woman looked at Stacy with interest. She smiled broadly and offered her hand, but her eyes remained cold as ice.

'Ah, you are a relative of Señor Moreno, I am told.' She turned to Felipe. 'You did not mention that you had an appointment, Felipe—I am sorry if I have kept you talking. You will have to come over to my house, we will have more time then.'

Luisa Aquilar was very beautiful, Stacy thought, but it was a cold, impersonal beauty—not a hair out of place, perfect make-up and a cold calculating look in her eyes. She decided that she was not the sort of woman to cross.

'How about tomorrow night?' she was saying. 'You could take me to the Yacht Club.'

Felipe shook his head. 'I'm sorry, Luisa, but I shall probably be taking Stacy somewhere tomorrow night.'

'Oh, I see, you are having to entertain your friend's relations. Well, never mind, perhaps another night, then?'

Felipe looked at her coldly. 'I'm not *having* to do anything, Luisa, it is a pleasure to take Stacy out, I do assure you.'

Luisa smiled politely. 'Of course, of course. You must give me a ring, when you are not committed, it had been such a long time since you took me any-where.'

'I must ask you to leave. I have kept Stacy waiting long enough,' he said icily.

'Very well, I will contact you later, when you are not entertaining your neighbours' children.'

'Goodbye,' Felipe said coldly. 'I doubt whether I shall be seeing you here again, or phoning you.' He turned his back on her, leaving her in no doubt that she had outstayed her welcome. He took Stacy's hand and walked away across the lawns, Luisa stood staring after them. He did not turn towards the villa, but headed for the cliff top. They did not speak until they reached it and Felipe sat down on an outcrop of rock and indicated that Stacy should do the same.

'Who was she?' Stacy asked in a thin voice.

'She was someone who saw a meal ticket taken

away from her,' he replied, 'and she wanted to make it unpleasant for the one who took it.'

'Was she your girl-friend?'

'No. She was an acquaintance, that's all. I took her out occasionally—when the mood took me. I did not give her up for you, if that is what you are thinking.'

'Did you make love to her?' Stacy couldn't help asking.

Felipe jumped up. 'Stacy!' he exclaimed, exasperated. 'You must not look at every woman to whom I speak and think I have been to bed with her.' He rubbed his hand through his hair. 'What I have done before is of no matter, it is now, we have to think forwards, not backwards.'

'I'm sorry. I'm jealous, that's all.'

He came down on his haunches beside her. 'Look, whatever I did before, I never told anyone I loved them—never. I have taken what was offered to me, like any normal man. I have let my body enjoy what was offered, but not my heart. That is yours, Stacy, all yours. Oh, I admit when I was younger I thought I had fallen in love on occasions, but it was never like this. This is like nothing I have ever felt before. Do you understand?'

He sounded so sincere, so tender, that Stacy burst into tears and he held her while she sobbed.

'Do not cry, *pequeña*,' he said softly into her hair. 'Luisa is a malicious woman, she likes to think she holds all the cards and she spits when she finds out that it is not so.'

He offered her his handkerchief and Stacy wiped her tear-stained face. He kissed her eyelids and then her mouth, but with only a gentle whisper across her lips which left her hungering for more.

'Hold me, Felipe,' she said tightly. 'Just hold me for a minute.'

He did so willingly.

Some time later they went down the winding steps to the beach and walked across the sand. They stood looking out across the wide blue bay. The sun was very hot and Felipe led her to a small bar on the beach where he ordered a jug of Sangria for them. They sat in the shade and drank silently for some time.

'I'm sorry I made a scene, Felipe,' said Stacy, fingering her glass, not daring to look at him.

'Let us forget it, shall we?' he replied. 'There is a barbecue in the next cove tonight, it is arranged by some friends of mine, would you like to go?'

'Oh yes, I'd love to. A barbecue,' she repeated wonderingly. 'I've never been to a proper one before.'

'Good, that is settled,' he replied, pouring another glass of Sangria.

She drank half the glass full in one go to quench her thirst.

'Hey!' Felipe cautioned, taking the glass from her fingers as she would have taken another swig, 'this is too strong to drink like lemonade. It is much more potent than you think. Take it easy—it is too hot to carry you all the way home!'

'I'm sure you could do it,' Stacy chided him.

'I should have your father to answer to—what would he think of me, carrying you home drunk at this time of day?'

'I think you'd feel the sharp edge of his tongue,' Stacy laughed. 'Dad always says what he thinks—whoever he's talking to.'

'You must take after your mother,' Felipe mused.

'Yes, I do,' Stacy told him. 'Why did you say that?'

'You are such a gentle creature,' he said, ruffling her hair. 'You are not at all like your father, he is much more down-to-earth. You are— —ethereal.'

'I've never been called that before,' Stacy laughed.

Felipe raised his glass to her and took a long drink.

'What time are we going out tonight?' she asked.

'I will pick you up at half past eight.'

'What shall I wear?'

'Whatever you like, it is not a formal occasion, just put on something you feel comfortable in.'

He stood up after looking at his watch and held out his hand to her. She took it, but instead of leaving the table he merely pulled her into his arms. 'All the time I want to touch you,' he said thickly, running his tongue gently across her forehead. As she lifted her face to look at him he kissed her hungrily and she reciprocated without restraint, even though there were other people sitting around them.

'Come on,' Felipe muttered, his arm around her shoulders, 'let's get you back. We will walk up the road instead of the steps, it is not so tortuous.'

Stacy dressed with care that night. She decided to wear a pair of harem trousers, coupled with a matching top with long full sleeves. The scooped neckline showed an expanse of now brown flesh and the dark pink material was a perfect foil for her blonde hair. She surveyed herself critically in the mirror. She looked slim in spite of the voluminous trousers and top, which was gathered in at the waist with a wide belt of the same material. Chris walked in and surveyed the picture before her.

'My goodness, that's striking. Where did you get it from?' she asked.

'I bought it from an Indian stall at the market in Birmingham,' Stacy replied. 'I've never had the courage to wear it before, although I've always fancied being able to.'

'Well, it's certainly worth wearing,' her sister replied. 'Felipe's downstairs—you'd better come down and dazzle him. He's having a drink with Fernando and Daddy.'

Felipe was indeed dazzled! As they got into the car he leaned over to shut her door and whispered, 'I think I will take you away somewhere, so that we can be on our own, instead of to the barbecue.'

Stacy looked at him wide-eyed. 'I don't mind.'

'Yes, you do,' he answered. 'You want to go to this barbecue, but I—well, I think I would like to lock you away in my harem.'

'I didn't know you kept one,' she laughed.

'I don't yet—but I could start. You would not mind being the only concubine, would you?'

'I wouldn't mind one bit—as long as I was the only one,' Stacy told him.

'Come, we had better get going. But later, then I shall get you on your own and then . . .' He curled an imaginary moustache, a wicked look on his face.

Stacy giggled. 'Come on, then.' She put her hand on his thigh and the car shot forward and stalled abruptly.

'Stacy, have pity on me, please! I have got to drive this thing after you have finished with me. At least let me keep some control.'

She removed her hand, laughing. It felt good to realise that just a touch of her hand could arouse him. She wanted to continue, just to see what effect it had, but thought better of it.

The barbecue was to be held at a large villa overlooking the bay on the other side from Felipe's house. They parked on a large grassy expanse at the side of the villa and Felipe took her hand as they walked over to where they could hear music and see the flickering lights on a wide crazy paved patio facing the sea. He took her over to a couple in their midthirties who were standing at the entrance to the patio, welcoming the guests as they arrived. They turned as Felipe and Stacy approached.

'Felipe!' exclaimed the small vivacious woman, grasping his hand with both of hers. 'I am so glad you could come!' She turned to Stacy and smiled at her warmly. 'This must be Stacy,' she said, holding out her hand. 'Felipe has told us all about you, my dear, we are so pleased to meet you.' She shook Stacy's hand and then put her own to her forehead. 'But first I should have introduced myself—I am so sorry. This is my husband José and I am Pilar, we are good friends of Felipe.'

'How do you do,' Stacy said politely, instantly taking a liking to Pilar. She was obviously well off, she could tell by the cut of her clothes alone—even without looking at the enormous villa in which she lived.

'You see,' Pilar told her, 'in honour of you we were told we must speak English, Felipe does not like to think that you cannot understand what is being said.'

'You speak it very well,' Stacy replied. 'But I do intend to learn Spanish as soon as I can. I've picked up a few words already.'

José then took her hand and shook it vigorously

with both of his. 'It is good to see you, Stacy,' he said in a mildly accented voice. 'I hope you will make Felipe very happy. He has certainly found a beautiful fiancée. I hope you will be very good for him.'

'I'll do my very best,' Stacy assured him.

Felipe coughed humorously. 'See,' he said, taking Stacy's hand, 'my friends are all concerned for my welfare!' He turned to José. 'She is not only beautiful to look at, she is beautiful to know, and that is more important.'

'Most definitely,' replied the older man, turning to his own wife. 'I hope you will find the happiness that we have found.'

'Come on, Felipe, Stacy,' Pilar broke in. 'This is getting too serious a conversation and tonight we are to be lighthearted. We are here to enjoy ourselves. Take Stacy over to the table and get her a drink, and yourself too. We have more guests coming, we must go and welcome them.'

'See you later,' Felipe said over his shoulder as he led Stacy towards the bar. There were wrought iron tables and chairs scattered all around the edges of the patio and a long low bar had been set up in one corner. At the opposite corner was an enormous charcoal grill and piles of chops and steaks piled up under glass-covered containers, ready to be cooked. The lights from the beach and the bar across from it reflected in the water beneath them, and Stacy watched with pleasure as the moon lighted up the scene below.

There were couples already dancing to a slow but rhythmic music played by a small band staged close to the house, and Felipe took her hand and led her on to the dance floor, wrapping his arms tightly around her as he did so.

'I haven't had a drink yet,' she complained.

'There is plenty of time for that,' he replied, looking down at her and smiling, 'but I want to dance with you, it is the only way I can get you into my arms with all these people about.'

She smiled up at him, her knees weakening at the feel of his thighs moving against her own. It wasn't really dancing, they merely turned around in circles enjoying the sensations which the close proximity afforded. When the music stopped they returned to their table and Felipe went to fetch a drink. He came back with a jug and two glasses and set them down carefully on the wrought iron table.

After the third glass Stacy was beginning to feel a little lightheaded.

'When do we have the food?' she asked bluntly. 'My head is starting to spin.'

'In about half an hour, I should think.' He stood up. 'Come with me, I think we might be able to find something to soak up the Sangria.'

He led her inside the wide open windows across the back of the villa and through a lounge which Stacy would have expected to see in a plush hotel. They found the kitchen and Felipe pushed her in in front of him.

'*Ola*, Juanita,' he said to one of the women preparing the food. She turned around and beamed at him, rattling off in rapid Spanish. Felipe replied in the same tongue and as if by magic a small plate of sandwiches appeared before Stacy. Felipe handed them to her and grinned. 'See what I can do if I try,' he said. 'All I have to do is ask and it is placed before me.'

'Yes,' said Stacy dryly, 'I bet it is.'

He looked down at her, wondering if he had read her words correctly, but the cheeky expression on her face told him that he had.

'Out,' he ordered pointing towards the door. 'I shall take you away and spank you for that remark—after you have eaten your sandwiches, of course!'

She giggled and walked back towards the kitchen door, smiling her thanks to the housekeeper for the sandwiches. Felipe led her to a room off the main hall. 'Here,' he said, 'you can eat here in peace.'

'Oh, I thought you'd brought me here to spank me,' Stacy countered, the wine making her more adventurous than she would normally have been.

'Do not tempt me, my darling. I think I might enjoy it. But it would lead to things that are best not carried out in a friend's house, especially while there is a party going on. I would prefer privacy.'

'So you keep telling me,' she replied, biting into another sandwich. 'These are delicious—do you want one?'

'You look much more appetising than the sandwiches,' he said, looking at her intently. 'Hurry up and finish them and we can get back outside before I am tempted to see if I am right.'

'Of course you are,' Stacy replied, her voice slightly slurred, 'and so are you—I mean, so are you delicious,' she explained. She ran a finger lightly down the front of his shirt and he grabbed at her hand, gasping.

'You are asking for trouble, *querida*,' he said huskily. 'I think you have drunk far too much on an empty stomach.'

'No, I haven't,' she replied. 'I haven't even started yet.'

'I think you had better eat some food before you

drink anything else. I find it hard to control you when you are in this mood.'

'Then why do you?' she asked.

'Next week, I will not try to, my love—next week; when you are mine, you may do whatever you want with me and I shall not stop you—I shall join you.'

She raised her lips and he took possession of them savagely, crushing her against him and letting her feel the effect she was having. She could feel him trembling in her arms and the power it gave her surged through her like a warm wave. He was muttering huskily in Spanish and she didn't know what he was saying, but his actions gave her a good idea. Suddenly she found herself flat on the couch with Felipe bearing down upon her. She could not remember getting there, but his hands on her body blotted out all sense of reality and she gave herself up to the sensations he was arousing. Her blouse was undone and she felt his lips burning across her exposed flesh like a trail of fire. She knew she could not stop him now, even if she had wanted to, and she abandoned herself to his lovemaking.

Suddenly a gong sounded, booming through the house and reverberating in their ears. Felipe was still and Stacy put her hands on either side of his face.

'It doesn't matter,' she croaked. 'They won't miss us, will they?'

But the spell was broken. Felipe was breathing heavily, his face a mask of pain at the thought of not completing what he had begun.

'Felipe, please,' she begged, but he got up from the couch and stood with his back to her, running a restless hand through his thick hair and round the back of his neck.

'Stacy, I am sorry, I should never have brought you in here—it was foolish. Please, get up—we must go and join the party.'

'But why?' she insisted.

He turned to her, his face a stern mask.

'You think I would deliberately insult my friends' hospitality by using it to seduce you on their sofa?' he questioned in a stony voice.

Stacy sat up then, quelled by his tone.

'I beg your pardon,' she replied, equally stonily, 'I didn't realise that was how you saw it. I thought you loved me.' His description of what they were doing had stung painfully and she wanted to retaliate.

Felipe gave an exasperated sigh. 'I do love you, very much, but I do not intend that your first time should be here on someone's sofa. Do you know what we should feel like afterwards, knowing what we had done? Dirty, cheap—it is the sort of thing you might do to a casual pick-up from the street who was willing, but not to someone you intend to marry. Come, we will be late.'

He opened the door and stood waiting for Stacy to precede him out. She rose woodenly and walked out on shaking legs, her head held high. Felipe caught her arm when she would have walked away from him and made her continue at his side. The smell of roasting meat filled their nostrils as they stepped out on to the patio and she realised that she was still hungry. The wine and Felipe's lovemaking had left an empty space in her stomach, and she headed for the tables where the food was being laid out.

'Ah, there you are,' said Pilar as they approached. 'Come on, Felipe, Stacy, you are our guests of honour, come and eat.'

Felipe picked up two plates and Stacy the cutlery. They walked slowly along the line of food, picking up delicious steak, sausages on sticks and baked potatoes and salad. They found a table to sit at and Stacy tucked into her steak with relish; she did not notice that Felipe was only picking at his.

A variety of people came to talk to Felipe, shaking his hand and patting him on the back in friendly fashion. He spoke to them all briefly and politely, but did not introduce Stacy to any of them. She presumed that they could not speak English and sat back to watch the proceedings, feeling a little annoyed.

A little later on a raven-haired sophisticate came waltzing over to their table and grabbed Felipe's hand, obviously wanting him to dance. Felipe spoke to her in Spanish and it was obvious to Stacy that he was trying to refuse, but the woman was very persistent. Eventually he stood up, shaking his head in annoyance. 'I will not be a moment, Stacy, wait here for me,' he said, and Stacy looked away angrily without replying. She was furious; how dared he leave her to dance with another woman! She did not sit alone for long, though. Within a few seconds she was being drawn to her feet by a handsome young Spaniard who pulled her on to the dance floor persuasively. Stacy had no intention of refusing. She was glad of an opportunity to pay Felipe back for his desertion.

'I am Antonio Rodriguez,' he told her. 'What is your name? I know you are English because I heard you speaking with Pilar earlier.'

'I'm Stacy Barker,' she replied.

'I like you, Stacy Barker,' he told her. 'I like you

very much.' He smiled down at her rakishly and pulled her a little closer, and Stacy put her hands on his chest to push him away. He continued to smile knowingly at her, getting nearer with every step, and she looked around in panic, trying to locate Felipe among the sea of people on the dance floor.

'What is the matter? Do you not like me?'

'I wanted to dance, nothing more,' Stacy told him coldly.

'Why? Are you worried about what your escort might say? Are you afraid that the wealthy Señor Cuevas will forget you and go home with someone else?'

'No,' Stacy replied with more confidence than she felt.

'Are you Felipe's latest conquest?' he asked. 'He has done well for himself this time, although he usually does. An English rose, no less!'

'English roses have thorns,' *señor*—you would do well to remember that!' Stacy snapped, trying unsuccessfully to extricate herself from his grip.

'I should very much enjoy removing your thorns, *amada*,' he replied with a wicked grin.

'Don't call me that!' Stacy said angrily. '*You* wouldn't get the chance to try, that's for certain!'

He pulled her hard against him and tried to kiss her, but she ducked away from him frantically. Suddenly a hard hand on her shoulder wrenched her away and a cold hard voice behind her shot out a spate of rapid Spanish at her captor.

'Surely you should speak in English in front of your lady friend,' Antonio Rodriguez said jeeringly. 'I am sure she would be most interested in the names you have just called me.'

'In future keep your hands off her or there will be

trouble,' Felipe replied unpleasantly. 'If you cannot find your own women you must go without—if you touch mine again I shall break every bone in your body!'

He swung Stacy around with little care for politeness and she stared into his stony face.

'What do you think you're doing?' he demanded, pulling her off the dance floor and pushing her roughly into a seat.

'What do *you* think *you're* doing, pushing me around like this?' she retorted angrily. 'I was dancing—the same as you were with that woman.'

'Oh no, not the same at all. I was dancing—you were virtually letting that pig make love to you on the dance floor.'

Stacy raised her hand as if to slap him, but thought better of it. Felipe, in his present mood, might think nothing of hitting her back.

'How dare you make such accusations! I was doing nothing of the sort!'

'I take my eyes off you for a minute and you turn to someone else . . .' Felipe muttered through his teeth.

'Oh no, let's get this right,' Stacy butted in. 'You mean you left me to dance with another woman, expecting me to sit waiting for you like an obedient puppy. If you were so concerned about me you wouldn't have rushed off and left me sitting there on my own among a load of strangers. He came over and asked me to dance. I saw nothing wrong in that—you were doing it—and *you* didn't ask *my* permission first. How was I to know he had something else in mind?'

'You should have come back to the table once you realised.'

'Oh yes, of course. I should suddenly develop the strength of Samson and push him away!' Stacy retorted, her voice raised in anger. 'Do you think I didn't try? If you'd been here it wouldn't have happened.' She drew a deep breath and turned away from him, picking up her drink and finishing it in one gulp.

'She would have pestered us all night if I had not explained the situation to her,' Felipe said by way of an explanation.

'So you had to dance with her to do it?'

'No, I didn't have to, but I thought it would be easier that way.'

'She shouldn't have even expected you to dance with her when you were with me—it was very rude.'

'I know, and I told her so.'

'O.K.—so you wanted to dance with her and I didn't want to sit here like a wallflower on my own— so I danced as well.'

'I would hardly call what you were doing dancing,' Felipe sneered.

Stacy gave him a scathing look. 'You can call it what you like,' she said crossly.

'I intend to.'

'I want to go home,' she said flatly.

'I do not want to,' he replied in an equal tone.

'Then I shall leave by myself,' she said, standing and picking up her bag.

His hand on her arm was like a vice.

'Let me go, will you! I don't want to stay here any longer,' she spat out, annoyed at her fragility and his strength.

'You will go when I say so and not before,' Felipe replied, not loosing his grip at all.

'I'm not your slave, who do you think you're

ordering about? I don't want to stay, sitting here being eyed up by all your friends and compared with all the others you've had.'

'What are you talking about?' he demanded. 'Did Rodriguez say something?'

'What does it matter? I know what they're all thinking. It was made very plain to me. I didn't realise you collected women like trophies,' she retorted angrily.

Felipe was annoyed, she could tell from the straight line of his lips and the once burning eyes were like chips of ice.

'Come,' he said, pulling her along behind him.

'Let me go!' she snapped. 'I can walk by myself, I don't need your help.'

But he ignored her and she was obliged to follow or cause a scene in front of all the other guests. He marched her over to their hosts and she heard him explaining that she had a headache and they were leaving. Seething, she managed to smile and thank the couple for their hospitality. Felipe stalked over to the car and opened the door, pushing her in roughly. Stacy tried to get out, but before she had mastered it he was beside her and his arm stretched across her to hold the door shut.

'I don't want to go with you!' she cried. 'Let me get out, who the hell do you think you are?'

'I am your fiancé, in case it slipped your mind, and I do not like what is mine flaunted about at my friends.'

'Flaunted—flaunted?' Stacy's voice was raised to fever pitch. 'How dare you say such a thing! If you have friends who see any woman as easy game and treat them as such that's not my fault. I can't get away from you when I want to, so how did you expect me to get away from him?'

Felipe started the engine and accelerated away in a cloud of dust. He did not speak again but drove at great speed away from the villa. Stacy realised almost immediately that they were not heading for home and she turned to him, startled.

'Where are you taking me?' she asked in a small, tight voice. She had never seen this side of him before, he had always treated her with respect, even when he was angry, but this stony-faced antagonist was new to her and frightening.

'Do not worry, I do not intend to drive over a cliff with you, or take you to some secluded spot and commit a dirty deed.'

'Then where are we going?' she persisted.

'Wait and see,' he replied noncommittally.

She gave an exaggerated sigh and rested her head on the back of the seat. Things had started out so well, she had looked forward to the evening, but now it had all gone wrong, over nothing at all!

Felipe turned into a small lane and the darkness shielded the countryside from her eyes as she looked around for any signs of where they were. It was a plateau, high above the sea, she realised when he stopped the car. In a fit of wild panic she managed to wrench the door open before he had time to stop her and fled away in the direction they had come. She should have known it would be futile, but desperation had made her reckless. She didn't like Felipe like this, and her only thought was escape.

She could hear him behind her; he called her name once, but she continued to run. A large stone hidden amongst the grass was her undoing. She tripped over it and fell heavily on the hard ground, landing in a heap. She heard Felipe cry out her name again, but was too stunned to move. Tears pricked her eyelids and she gave herself up to them.

Within seconds he was on his knees beside her, his hands, now gentle, on her shoulders trying to turn her over.

'Stacy, are you all right? Stacy, answer me!'

She groaned and huddled up into a tighter ball.

'Stacy,' he begged, 'answer me—are you hurt?'

'Go away,' she managed in a stifled voice. 'Leave me alone!'

'Don't be silly, I want to know if you are hurt—tell me,' he insisted.

'Only by you,' she told him.

'Can you move? You have not broken anything?' he asked, ignoring her last remark. When she did not answer he gently but purposefully grasped her shoulders and lifted her up into a sitting position. 'If you lie there you will ruin your clothes, and it would be a pity to spoil that outfit. Come, let us go back to the car,' he said in a persuasive voice.

Stacy was unresponsive and before she realised his intention he lifted her up into his arms and carried her effortlessly back. She was too tired to fight, and his nearness and the smell of his aftershave and cheroots made her want to relax against him and pretend their argument had never happened. He sat her in her seat and closed the door. Moving lithely around the hood to his own side, he eased himself behind the wheel and turned to her.

'I am sorry if I upset you, *querida*,' he apologised in a quiet voice. He took hold of her chin and turned her to face him. 'I am a jealous man,' he began, 'when I saw you dancing with that . . . well, anyway, when I saw you I just saw red. You do not know what an intimate little scene it seemed to be.'

'But it wasn't,' Stacy told him. 'I was trying to get away from him, but he wouldn't let me go. He . . . he said I was your latest conquest . . . it made me feel—cheap—cheap!' she repeated, flinging the word in his face.

'You should not have listened to him. You should have realised he was baiting you and ignored him.'

'Ignored him? How could I ignore him when he had me in a stranglehold? You didn't let me ignore you when you met me in Chris's garden the other night, did you?'

'That was different,' he retorted immediately.

'Oh yes, of course it was different. That was you holding me back, wasn't it? I can't be held responsible for other people's actions whether they're yours or anybody else's.'

There was silence for a few seconds.

'Point taken,' Felipe answered flatly. 'I say again—I am sorry.'

'Why did you go off with that woman and leave me stranded? That didn't seem to trouble you very much. If you can do it I see no reason why I shouldn't,' Stacy asked angrily.

'I—she—she was just an old acquaintance, I didn't want her hanging around our necks all night. I thought that was the best way to get rid of her,' he replied.

'Well, that sounds a feeble excuse,' Stacy stated. 'If you're embarrassed by knowing me you only have to say. I get the distinct impression that you're hiding me away, that you don't want anyone to know. I wonder why?'

'If I keep people from you it is for your own good. You see what happens when you are left alone for a few moments. Someone says something you do not like and it hurts you. I shall make sure that Rodriguez pays for his misdemeanour!'

'What do you mean?', Stacy asked, startled by the tone of his voice.

Felipe shrugged his shoulders noncommittally. 'Nothing for you to worry about. He is a business competitor of mine, I think I would like to make things a little difficult for him.'

'That's a terrible thing to do!' Stacy shouted. 'Just because he danced with me—who do you think you are? You would make life very pleasant for me, I can see—walking around afraid to speak to anyone in case you took exception to it—well, no, thanks, if that's the way it's going to be then you can keep it!'

She attempted to remove the ring from her finger, but Felipe's hand gripped hers to stop her.

'Oh no, you don't,' he said, his other hand drawing her towards him determinedly. Stacy struggled to avoid him, but it was impossible. He pushed her back against the seat with his body and kept her pinioned there, staring into her outraged face with a cynical smile playing on his lips.

'You have a fiery temper for one who looks so sweet,' he told her softly, his eyes lowered to look at her mouth.

'No,' she managed to say, before his lips met hers with fierce impact.

After a few breathtaking minutes he raised his head. 'Oh yes. I told you before—now that you wear my ring you are mine. I will never let you go. You had your chance to refuse, but you accepted me. There is no turning back now.'

He didn't give her time to reply, but kissed her again. Stacy forced herself to remain impassive, closing her lips tightly and making herself as stiff as she could under his demanding hands. She could tell he was becoming angry at her lack of response and waited despairingly for him to push her away. She ached to wrap her arms around him and hold him to her, but pride would not allow it.

Suddenly his tactics changed. His kisses became light and feathery across her eyes and cheeks. His tongue traced the line from her ear to her chin. His hands caressed her ceaselessly, but gently, making her tingle from head to foot. He took her earlobe between his teeth and teased it until she writhed beneath him. 'Kiss me,' he demanded hoarsely, and she was too weak then to disobey. At last she gave way to her passion, wrapping her arms about him and kissing him back hungrily.

'I am not ashamed of you,' Felipe whispered into her neck. 'Never think that. Only a fool would feel so; you are everything I ever wanted, ever will want. But I am afraid of losing you and I can't bear the thought of another man touching you.' He took her mouth again with a savage passion which underlined his previous words. Stacy was carried away on the tide of emotion, uncaring any more for the things which they had said and done a few hours previously. He was all that mattered, she was his, with all the problems which that entailed.

Felipe released her at last, his breath ragged and his body shaking. He slumped over the wheel and put his head down on the cool surface. Stacy lay back in her seat, drained yet still unsatisfied. The silence was broken only by the chirruping of crickets in the long grass. At last Felipe turned back to her.

'Let us forget what happened, *querida*, and start again. I will try to keep my temper, but promise me

you will not get involved with anyone but me.
Promise?'

'I promise, Felipe,' she replied. 'You mis-
understood the situation, that's all. I've never
wanted anyone else but you—you should know that.'

'I knew I should have waited, given you time to
make your decision, but God help me, I could not
wait,' he said in a tortured voice.

'Please,' Stacy begged, 'don't let's talk about it
any more, Felipe. I know exactly what I want, I
don't need time to decide—I already have. Let's just
forget it ever happened—the argument, I mean—
shall we?'

'Of course,' he replied, looking down at her
lovingly. He kissed her on the top of her nose and
released his hold. After a few seconds he started the
car and drove off quite slowly across the grassy
headland.

Through the darkness, the lights of a small bar
appeared in the distance and Felipe asked her if she
would like a drink to finish off the evening.

'Lovely,' Stacy replied.

He pulled up outside and stilled the engine. 'It
will be nothing special,' he told her. 'It is probably
the haunt of local farmers.'

'I don't mind.'

Felipe drew aside the bead curtain which served
as a door and took Stacy's hand as they walked in.
All eyes turned as they made their way across to the
bar and she smiled shyly to cover her embarrassment. Felipe ordered her a drink, and one for himself, and looked around for a table to sit at. Someone
in the far corner shouted and he led the way over to
where the man had indicated.

'I'm the only woman here,' Stacy whispered.

'I am sure they do not mind that,' Felipe told her, taking her hand under the table.

One old man passed their table with a couple of overflowing beers in his hands. He stopped and spoke to Felipe, grinning toothlessly at Stacy before moving on.

'What did he say?' she asked quietly.

'He said I was a very lucky man to have such a beautiful wife. They are simple people here, but they appreciate beauty when they see it.'

'You're embarrassing me,' Stacy replied.

'You should not be embarrassed, you should be proud of your beauty—I know that I am.'

She smiled demurely and rested her head on his shoulder. Someone near the bar started singing and before long the whole of the tiny bar had joined in. Stacy looked around in astonishment.

'It is nearly time to go home,' Felipe explained. 'They are all making the most of the last few minutes—enjoying an old folk song together.'

'What time is it, then?' she asked.

'It is nearly two o'clock,' he told her, peering carefully at his watch in the dim lighting.

'Two o'clock? I didn't realise it was so late!'

'It has been an eventful evening,' Felipe said with wry humour.

'You can say that again!'

'I am truly sorry for my loss of temper, *querida*,' he told her. 'I do not usually lose control so easily. You bring out the best and the worst in me.'

'I'm sorry I was so jealous,' Stacy admitted. 'It was only because you went off to dance with that woman that I did the same. Normally I wouldn't have accepted.'

He squeezed her hand. 'I am glad to know I can

make you jealous too,' he said. 'But you should never feel that way. I have eyes for nobody but you—ever since the day I met you.'

'Good, I like it like that,' Stacy said truthfully.

'I think it is time we went home,' Felipe said on a sigh. 'You are beginning to look very tired, *querida*.'

'I'm beginning to feel it,' she replied.

'We have many things to talk about if we are to be married soon. You must get some rest and be alert tomorrow so we can discuss our plans.'

'At the moment I feel anything *but* alert,' she said candidly. 'But I promise you I will be tomorrow, especially if we're going to discuss our wedding plans.'

Felipe kissed her on the nose again and guided her out of the crowded bar. Stacy was surprised when all its inhabitants called out, wishing them goodnight as they left.

The drive home was tedious in the dark and she could not keep her eyes open. She was so tired that she did not even wake up when Felipe reached the villa and parked outside. The house was in darkness, obviously at that late hour they were all in bed. Felipe looked down at Stacy's reclining figure and sighed. He opened the front door quietly and pushed it back before carefully removing the sleeping girl from the car and carrying her slowly up the stairs to her room.

CHAPTER FIVE

IT was nine o'clock when Stacy woke the following morning. She sat up in bed and pondered on how she had arrived there. She realised she still had on her bra, and then remembered that she had had to wear it with her blouse the previous evening as the material was slightly see-through. With a shrug of her shoulders she threw back the light covers and got up, stretching lazily. She had just put on her housecoat when a knock came at the door.

'Are you awake, Stacy?' her sister's voice called.

'Yes,' she replied. 'Come in, Chris, I've just got up.'

'Ah, at last—I looked in earlier, but you were dead to the world. I take it you enjoyed your evening out?'

'Oh, yes, thank you, it was very good. Chris, what do you think now? Surely you don't think Felipe's having me on, do you? He wouldn't go this far, would he?'

Chris shrugged. 'How should I know? I'm afraid you're far too immature to hold Felipe for long, Stacy. You've let him drag you into his trap. I did warn you . . . anyway, it's done now, and Fernando has forbidden me to say any more on the subject. I just hope you know what you're letting yourself in for, that's all.'

'Chris,' Stacy pleaded, 'why are you so against it? I can't see . . .'

'No, that's just the trouble,' Chris interrupted,

'you can't. Now, you'd better get dressed. Felipe is downstairs; anyone would think he hadn't got a home of his own to go to.' She walked to the door and stopped. 'Don't go mentioning anything to him or Fernando, will you? I'm only thinking of you. Fernando doesn't know, you see, he thinks Felipe is perfect. He doesn't know what we do.'

She left the room, and Stacy stared at the closed door.

Felipe was already sitting by the pool when Stacy arrived there. He rose as she stepped through the french windows and kissed her as she reached him.

'You do not look well, *querida*. What is wrong?'

'Felipe, I have to talk to you, in private, now.'

'What is wrong?' he repeated.

'Can we go to your house to talk? Chris and Fernando will be out soon.'

'Of course,' he said, leading the way.

When they reached the villa he showed her into his study and offered her a seat. Stacy shook her head, and Felipe frowned at her, curious at her agitation.

'Well, *querida*, what is the matter?' he asked softly.

'I can't go through with it, Felipe. I can't marry you,' she said, her words tripping over each other.

His expression changed from utter shock to boiling anger in a few short seconds. 'What do you mean? You can't marry me—just like that, after we have become engaged? Why? I know it has all happened quickly, but yesterday you were so sure, why is today different?'

'Felipe, I can't explain—please, can't you just accept it?'

He let out an expletive and grasped her arm. 'Just

accept it, with no explanation, no apology? Of course I cannot just accept it. You are a fool if you thought I would. What was this, some sort of game? Something to pass the time while you were on holiday? If it's because I was angry with you yesterday why not say so?'

Stacy shook her head. 'It isn't that, Felipe. I . . . I . . .'

'What is it, then?' he demanded, shaking her. 'Something must have happened, you cannot just change your mind overnight without a reason.'

'I—I think perhaps it would be a mistake—I don't really know you properly and you don't know me. It's better to find out now than wait until it's too late.'

'What are you talking about? This is nonsense— we have been through it before, but last time you told me that if you loved me enough, which you assured me you did, everything would be fine. How has that situation changed?'

Stacy was regretting her insistence on privacy. Felipe looked mutinous and the grip he had on her arms was painful.

'Please let me go, Felipe, you're hurting me,' she said plaintively, but he ignored her request.

'Not half as much as you are trying to hurt me, Stacy, I assure you of that,' he told her.

She sighed deeply, biting her bottom lip to stop herself from crying. 'I didn't mean to hurt you, Felipe, I swear I didn't.'

'You do not love me any more, is that it? You did not ever love me, then?'

Stacy wanted to lie, to say that she had no feelings for him, but the look on his face and the pain in his eyes was more than she could stand. She looked up at him and he could read her feelings clearly in her face. He pulled her hard against him, finding her mouth and parting the soft lips before she could escape. His kiss was desperate, his hands agitated as they moulded her to him.

'For God's sake, Stacy, don't do this to me,' he whispered huskily, kissing her face and neck rapidly.

'Felipe,' she moaned, 'oh, Felipe!'

He held her tightly against him and she could feel his trembling body down the whole length of her own.

'Stacy, tell me what is wrong? I will reassure you, whatever it is.'

She closed her eyes tightly and tried to clear her fuzzy mind. She had promised Chris she would not mention her outburst earlier and she would not go back on her word. It was obvious that Felipe would never admit the accusations, even if she confronted him with them. He always had an answer to everything.

'I—I just thought that perhaps you would get tired of me after a while—that you'd regret having married me so quickly,' she lied. 'You come from a totally different background—I wouldn't fit in, Felipe.'

He held her away from him to look into her face. 'What do you think I am?' he asked. 'I do not find it necessary to flit from woman to woman like a bee in a flower garden. I am quite capable of staying faithful to you, Stacy, I would never have asked you to marry me if I wasn't so sure. Who has been putting doubts into your mind?'

'No one,' she assured him. 'No one at all.' She could feel herself blushing at her lies. 'I'm sorry, Felipe, perhaps I'm just being stupid.'

'Indeed you are, *querida*. My background has nothing to do with how I feel for you or how you feel for me. What difference will it make? When we are married all that is mine will be yours also. My background will be yours. Tell me that you have not changed your mind. Tell me that you will marry me.'

'Oh yes, Felipe, I will. I'm so sorry for being stupid.'

'So you should be! Kiss me—I think I deserve a kiss after the torment you have just subjected me to.'

Some time later they began to discuss the wedding plans. Stacy agreed to leave all the arrangements to Felipe. They agreed on a quiet wedding with only a few people in attendance, and Stacy insisted that they should be married in Menorca.

'I'd love it to be here, Felipe,' she told him. 'Is it possible?'

'I would have thought you would have preferred England,' he replied thoughtfully.

'No. I met you here and I'd like to marry you here. It's such a lovely place—an ideal setting, don't you think?'

Felipe shrugged, rubbing his fingers around his chin. 'If that is what you want, I will see if it can be arranged. We will have to keep it very quiet, thought. I am well known around here, and we don't want half the island turning up, do we?'

'Oh, lovely—thank you, darling!' Stacy exclaimed, clapping her hands together like a child. 'It would be silly to trudge all the way back to England when we're all here now, a complete waste of time and money.'

'Very well, that is settled,' Felipe said, drawing

her down on to his lap. His actions were more of a father to a child than a man to his future wife, and Stacy cuddled up to him tantalisingly.

He pushed her a little away from him. 'Do not torment me at this time of day. I have suffered enough. I have to think clearly, and you do not make it easy for me.'

Stacy pulled a face at him. 'Spoilsport!' she teased.

'Tomorrow I must go and sort out my business,' he told her seriously. 'I have to clear up all the loose ends before our wedding, make sure that everything runs smoothly while we are away. I do not want anything to interrupt our honeymoon. While I am away I would like you to go to Paris and choose a wedding dress. I'm sure Chris would accompany you.'

Stacy pushed away from him. 'Paris? Haven't you got any shops in Mahón that sell wedding dresses?'

He laughed softly. 'I want you to have the best. I thought you would be pleased—you will only get the chance once to wear a wedding gown. There will be more of a selection in Paris.'

'But it'll cost a fortune!' Stacy argued.

He put a finger on the tip of her nose, his expression stern. 'You will have to learn not to argue with me about money. I know what I can afford. When you are my wife I shall beat you soundly if you argue with me over it.'

'You wouldn't dare!' Stacy replied.

'Oh, wouldn't I? Just wait and see. If you do not behave yourself I shall begin now.' He stood up, holding Stacy in his arms as if she weighed nothing. He put her down gently beside him and took her hands. 'I will make you happy, *querida*, I promise. Never doubt me again.'

Stacy smiled up at him. I'm sure you will, Felipe. It's just that when I'm not with you I start worrying. I'm quite certain now we're together.'

He shook his head. 'Women!' he exclaimed, walking over to his desk and leaning against it. 'I will give you some money for your dress and arrange for my secretary to have it changed and ready for you at the airport with your tickets and hotel reservations. You do not need to worry over anything. It will all be planned in advance.'

'No wonder you're such a good business man,' Stacy told him. 'You don't give any one else a look in, do you?'

'You are not happy with the arrangements? I thought it would occupy your time until I returned.'

'I will see you before the wedding, won't I? I don't think I could stand not seeing you before then,' Stacy asked suddenly.

'But of course you will, *querida*. I shall be back on Thursday and as soon as I arrive I will come to see you. But now, I will take you to a fiesta—would you like that?'

'Oh yes—a real fiesta?'

'Certainly a real fiesta. I must officiate there, I'm afraid—make a speech. But it will not take long and we can enjoy ourselves afterwards.'

'What happens, Felipe, what is it like?' Stacy asked.

'There will be a band playing on a platform outside the civic building and all the villagers have a holiday. They dress up in their finery and come with the intention of enjoying themselves. The young men of the village will test out their skill on horseback. They ride around the square and rear their horses up at the crowd. The locals also test their nerves and dive underneath the horses' hooves as they rear up. It is quite a spectacle.'

'It sounds dangerous to me!' Stacy commented.

'Not really—the horsemen are competent, and the horses are very careful also.'

'What else happens?'

'There are many stalls and sideshows for us to wander around. They usually sell cheap trinkets, but it is fun to buy such things at a fiesta.'

'I can't wait!' she smiled.

'Good. It is very hot today, go and fetch your hat and we will go.'

Stacy hurried over to the villa and collected her straw hat, the one Felipe had bought her when she first arrived. She told her father where she was going and kissed him affectionately before running back to Felipe's villa.

'I'm ready,' she told him breathlessly.

'You should not have rushed, we have plenty of time,' Felipe assured her.

'I wanted to get back to you,' she said, taking his hand.

A smile lit up his face. 'An admirable sentiment, *querida*,' he replied. 'Come on, then, let us go.'

The journey to San Jaime was uneventful and Felipe spent the time telling Stacy about the fiesta of San Juan which took place every year in Ciudadela.

'Fiestas date from the Middle Ages,' he said. 'Each one is slightly different, although the principles are the same. On the Sunday before the fiesta of San Juan a group of *caixers* preceded by a man dressed in furs go as an entourage to invite people to the fiesta. The man in furs always carries a live lamb on his shoulders. There are many different traditions.'

'It all sounds fantastic,' Stacy enthused. 'I wonder why we don't have them in England?'

'You have carnivals,' Felipe replied.

'Oh yes, but we don't get a day off to go to them or anything. We don't make such a fuss of things as you do. I prefer your way.'

'That is good,' Felipe replied, casting a quick glance at her. 'You will be involved in all these things when you become my wife. I always go home for the fiesta in our own village. It is expected of me. The villagers work hard in the vineyards and olive groves all the year. When it is fiesta time they let themselves go, but they like to see their employer taking an interest in them—it is only fair. They will be glad to know that at last I am taking a wife who will give me strong sons to carry on working the estate and keeping their own children in employment. They will welcome you with open arms.'

Stacy blushed prettily. 'We may not have any sons, we could have daughters,' she said.

'In my family we always have sons,' Felipe said confidently.

'Well, we'll have to wait and see,' Stacy reasoned. 'Oh, look, is that where the fiesta is?'

She pointed to a wide square in front of them. There was a lawn in the middle, covered in stalls, and bunting fluttered in the breeze. There were people everywhere, fanning themselves against the heat or relaxing on the grass. Sleek black horses bedecked in ribbons and finery shuffled impatiently in a small courtyard, small children ran around with ice creams or sticky candy sticks, all taken up with the party spirit.

'It's so colourful,' Stacy said as Felipe carefully parked his car next to the civic building.

'It will also be very hot—you must not allow yourself to get sunstroke, *querida*. Put your hat on immediately.'

She did as she was told and Felipe kissed her lightly before getting out of the car.

'Come, we must make our presence known to the Mayor. He should be over by the rostrum.'

They walked across the crowded square and up on to the platform which housed a motley selection of musicians, ready to play their hearts out in the tremendous heat for the sake of the fiesta. The Mayor in all his finery came towards them and shook Felipe's hand and then Stacy's. He knew no English, except for 'Good morning', which he repeated over and over again to her—quite pleased with himself for knowing at least two words of English.

'You must learn our language quickly, my darling, you will be able to join in the conversation then,' observed Felipe.

'Yes,' Stacy replied, 'I'd like to. You'll have to teach me.'

'I shall look forward to it,' he told her. 'Now, let's get the proceedings under way.'

Stacy stood back as he went to the front of the platform to make his opening speech. She was amazed that the noisy crowds were immediately silent, except for a few crying babies, as he began. She could understand nothing of what was being said, but she was quite content to watch him, marvelling at his extreme confidence. He was finished very soon and came back to stand with her, taking her hand and squeezing it as the Mayor stepped forward.

'I do not believe in long speeches,' he told her. 'The people come to enjoy themselves, they are too restless and it is far too hot for them to stand still for long. The *jaleo* will start soon—that is the horse display I was telling you about.'

Soon afterwards, as Felipe had said, the horses came from the courtyard across the square. Their grooming was immaculate and their riders were obviously revelling in the attention they would get for the day. Stacy marvelled at their antics, each one trying to outdo the previous rider in skill and daring. They reared their horses up at the crowd, who cheered and encouraged each one enthusiastically. Stacy's camera was clicking away all the time, recording the gaiety and colourfulness of the occasion.

'You will need a room to keep all these photographs in,' Felipe laughed. 'You haven't stopped since the fiesta began.'

'But it's great, Felipe. Dad would love to see these snaps, I'm sure.'

Felipe looked serious. 'Yes, I suppose we should have offered to bring him with us, but I am afraid I was too selfish—I wanted you to myself. I am sorry, *querida.*'

Stacy shook her head slowly. 'You don't have to be, I want to be with you too.'

He squeezed her hand again and pointed to where another rider was impressing the crowds with his skills on horseback.

When the *jaleo* was over they descended from the platform and mingled with the crowds. Felipe bought Stacy an enormous ice cream and took a photograph of her trying to eat it before it melted all over her hand. They walked slowly around the stalls, laughing and joking with the stallholders and buying silly trinkets to remind them of the day. Eventually they felt too hot to stay longer in the crowded square and Felipe led Stacy through the narrow streets and down to the harbour where they were sheltered from the sun by the sandy cliffs.

Stacy sat on the edge of the path and dangled her hot feet in the cool water while Felipe took off his tie and unbuttoned his shirt.

'Mmmm, I love the sun,' Stacy said eventually. 'I could stay here for ever.'

'I think you would get hungry, *pequeña*. In fact, I am feeling hungry now. Shall we find somewhere to eat?'

'That would be nice. I didn't think about it until you mentioned it, but now I feel hungry too.'

Felipe offered her his hand and pulled her to her feet. Stacy stood on tiptoe and kissed him.

'I've really enjoyed today, Felipe. Thank you for bringing me.'

'It has been my pleasure. I should not have enjoyed it without you. I suppose we had better go back and say our farewells to the officials before we go for our lunch. It would be rude to go without.'

After they had shaken hands with everybody on the platform Felipe led Stacy away through the crowds and back to the car.

'I think we had better go elsewhere for our meal. Villa Carlos will be far too crowded for us to get anything. How about Bini Beca—you liked it there, didn't you?'

'Oh yes, to the little pub again, that would be lovely,' Stacy agreed.

'Well—actually, I thought we might have a picnic. We still have a lot to say to each other. I would like to be alone with you.'

Stacy found it hard to swallow. 'That sounds even better,' she managed to say.

They bought some rolls and meat from the inn-keeper and a bottle of lemonade to drink and walked over the rocks to a small beach which was deserted at that time of day. Felipe found a sheltered spot and they sat down and spread out the travelling rug.

'I can't believe I'm going to Paris for my wedding dress,' Stacy mused. 'It doesn't seem five minutes since I was getting very nervously on to that plane to bring me out here to see Chris. Just think, I didn't even know you existed then. I can't think how I ever managed without you.'

Immediately his eyes burned into hers. 'The feeling is mutual,' he told her softly.

'Oh, Felipe, I do love you,' Stacy told him simply, running her soft hand down the side of his face.

'And I you,' he returned.

'Well, kiss me, then,' she said, 'because I feel very unsure of myself at the moment. Reassure me, Felipe.'

'But why should you feel like this?' Felipe queried.

'I just feel safer when I'm with you.' She paused thoughtfully. 'I just wish I didn't have to go away from you, that's all.'

'But it is only for two days—surely you trust me? There is nothing to be afraid of. I need to make arrangements, you must understand this. Not only the wedding, but also my business commitments—I want to take you away for a honeymoon without having to worry about such things. You are surely not changing your mind again, Stacy—tell me?'

'No, of course not,' she assured him.

He gave an involuntary gasp and held her in his arms.

'Stacy, you must trust me. You must feel confident enough in yourself to know that I would never do anything to jeopardise our relationship. Just remember that and everything will be all right.'

He kissed her, and all thoughts but those of his touch left her mind.

After their picnic Felipe cleared up the papers they had used as serviettes and also the wrapping paper from the rolls and they walked slowly back to the car.

At the villa Stacy clung to him as he was about to leave and he tried desperately to comfort her. 'Two days, *querida*—only two days. We have a whole lifetime in front of us after that.'

Stacy tried hard to cheer herself up. It seemed like an eternity; she could not think of life without him now.

CHAPTER SIX

THEY arrived in Paris early on Wednesday morning. Chris had agreed to accompany Stacy, but although she tried hard to conceal it, Stacy knew she was not happy about her impending marriage. This made Stacy uneasy and she had tried repeatedly to discuss the matter with her sister, but Chris had refused point blank to enter into such a conversation. It was obvious that Fernando had spoken to her after her last outburst and she would not go against his wishes.

They unpacked their overnight bags and, after a

quick wash and brush up, they went to the Metro which would take them to the shops. Stacy was in a trance. She had never been to Paris before and her stunned senses, which had had to cope with quite a few new situations in the last few weeks, could not register properly.

'I know I'm here,' she told Chris, 'but I can't believe it.'

Chris whisked her straight to an exclusive fashion house, obviously recommended by Felipe, and they sat in sumptuous surroundings watching the mannequins parading before them. Stacy set her heart on the third dress displayed to her. It was not too ornate but extremely feminine, with a high neck and fitted bodice, tight-fitting lacy sleeves and a waterfall effect full skirt. She tried it on and, apart from a few minor alterations, it looked perfect. She looked at Chris for confirmation, and she nodded her approval. 'Oh yes, that looks lovely, Stacy, you need look no further. It could have been designed for you.'

The vendeuse clapped her hands together in delight and told 'Madame' it was *magnifique*. They were told that the alterations would be carried out immediately and the dress would be sent to their hotel by six o'clock. Stacy then examined shoes and headdresses to go with her dress and decided on a pretty white flowered headdress. At the centre of each flower was a sparkling imitation diamond, and the single layer veil which went with it looked superb.

She left the building almost in tears—everything was so beautiful, she knew she would feel spectacular in such adornments. She only hoped that Felipe would approve her choice. She had not asked the price of anything and none had been offered with price tags on them, so she was completely ignorant of the cost of anything she had purchased. Chris had taken care of all that, talking quietly to the vendeuse, out of Stacy's hearing.

They decided to have lunch before looking for accessories and a going away outfit, and chose a pleasant open-air café which served a delicious cold table. It was after six o'clock when they eventually returned to their hotel. A porter appeared with a trolley and unloaded the taxi for them. Back in their room they fell on to their respective beds, exhausted.

'Well,' said Chris, looking at the pile of parcels on the table by the window, 'that's a good day's work. I bet you've never done that sort of shopping before—never having to ask the price, I mean.'

'No, you're right,' Stacy replied. 'And I feel very guilty about that. Felipe says he'll spank me if I mention the cost of things, but I was brought up that way—I can't change overnight.'

'No, I'm sure you can't,' Chris replied off-handedly.

Stacy did not want to start that sort of discussion with her sister and changed the subject immediately.

'You'll look great in that suit—so sophisticated. Fernando will love it.'

Chris laughed. 'No one will be looking at me, darling—you'll be the star attraction on that day.'

'Well,' Stacy persisted, 'Fernando will love you whatever you wear.'

'Yes, good old Fernando, I suppose he would.'

Dinner took them a long time. Stacy talked incessantly and could not concentrate wholeheartedly on her food.

'Felipe says we can go to the Greek islands for

our honeymoon. He has a friend who owns one—an island, I mean—and he says we can use it for our honeymoon.'

Chris nodded, but did not reply.

'I can't believe I'm getting married,' Stacy giggled. The bottle of wine which accompanied the meal had made her lightheaded, although she noticed Chris had drunk most of it. 'It's all happened so quickly,' she continued.

Chris took another sip of wine. 'You're telling me,' she said. 'You come over here to spend a holiday with me and go off with the next door neighbour— even after I'd warned you he was not to be trusted. I don't think I'd fancy marrying a man who'd tried to make love to *my* sister—I'd never be sure he wouldn't try it again.'

Stacy looked up, horrified, her eyes brimming with tears.

'Chris, that's a terrible thing to say! You must have got it wrong—I don't think Felipe is like that.'

'Oh, right, so I'm a liar as well, I suppose. Well, please yourself, but don't say I didn't warn you.'

'Why are you being so bitchy towards me?' asked Stacy worriedly. 'I don't know what's the matter with you—you never used to be like this. Do you fancy Felipe yourself or something?'

Chris gave a brittle laugh. 'Fancy him? Huh! It's the other way around, darling, he's made it quite plain that *he* fancies *me*. He's probably only marrying you because he can't have me. Heaven knows, he's made it quite obvious that he wants me.'

'*No!*' Stacy gasped. 'It's not true!'

'Oh yes, it is,' said Chris, her voice a little slurred. 'I had to threaten to tell Fernando before he'd stop. And you go and throw yourself at him as soon as he crooks his finger. I didn't think you were such a fool, Stacy. Well, if it's just his money you're after I suppose you could do a lot worse. Still, I wouldn't want to risk it.'

'Chris, please, don't speak to me like this,' Stacy begged.

'You need someone to bring you to your senses, darling. Has he told you about his previous fiancée yet? Has he told you that his mother will probably throw a fit when she finds out he's married an English girl—and behind her back as well? Didn't it cross your mind that it was a bit strange to just rush off and get married without meeting his family first?'

'He explained all that to me,' Stacy tried to defend herself.

'Oh yes, I'm sure he has. Our Felipe has a way with words, he'd make you believe black was white—and you're too stupid to see through it.'

Stacy stood up abruptly, tears streaming down her face. She knocked over her chair and ran from the dining room, uncaring of the scene she was making. Chris followed.

'Where do you think you're going?' she called to Stacy.

'Leave me alone,' Stacy sobbed, 'just go away and leave me alone!'

'I'm sorry, Stacy, but I hate to see you waste your life on someone like Felipe. Why don't you find someone in your own class?'

'Like you did, I suppose?' Stacy countered.

'Fernando's not like Felipe and never will be—surely you realise that?'

'I don't realise anything—just leave me alone. I'm going for a walk—don't wait up for me.'

She turned and ran out of the side entrance of the

hotel and into the garden. She could never remember how long she spent on the ornamental
bridge which straddled a small stream, staring
blindly at the gurgling water below. It crossed her
mind to fall in and hold her head beneath the shal-
low water, but her common sense prevailed.

It was past two o'clock when she walked back into
the hotel. Anyone seeing her would have thought
she was sleepwalking. She was pale and her eyes
stared straight ahead, walking seemed to be an effort.
She entered the bedroom quietly. Chris was fast
asleep. Stacy moved about, packing her overnight
bag and removing the money which Felipe had
given her to spend, placing it in a hotel envelope
and leaving it on Chris's table. She caught a
glimpse of herself in the bathroom mirror—the face
looking back at her was wild, almost insane. 'I
can't possibly look like that,' she thought fleetingly.
She turned away; what difference did it make any
more what she looked like?

Everything Chris had said made some sort of
sense. Felipe had told her that he didn't want to
introduce her to his family until after the wedding;
would they really have accepted her with open
arms, as he had said? She doubted it now. Chris
was her sister, there was no possible reason for her
to lie.

'Ham roll, love, and how about a date tonight?' the
young labourer asked, leaning over the counter.

Stacy ignored the last remark, her face blank.
'Ham roll,' she repeated, removing one from the
glass case beside her.

The young man shrugged, instinct warning him
that he was wasting his time on her.

'Thirty pence, please. Do you want tea or coffee?' Stacy asked politely.

'Coffee, please, love, two sugars.'

'The sugar is on the table.'

After putting the money in the till she ran a tired hand over her face. Working in a café had seemed a good idea two weeks ago when she had returned to England. She had been lucky to find a job at all, she repeatedly told herself, but her aching feet and legs repudiated that assumption. The people who owned the establishment had been very kind—northerners who were working in London to earn enough to retire comfortably to their bungalow in Dorset. Stacy had walked into their café on the day she arrived from Paris, weary and thoroughly dejected. She had looked so miserable that Mrs Johnson, a small plump lady with a heart of gold, had come over to her to see if she was all right. Her kindness had been Stacy's undoing and, in their lounge at the back of the café, she had sobbed out her story—or some of it—to Mrs Johnson's receptive ears.

They had insisted that she stay in their upstairs flat and also offered to give her a job serving in the café if she wanted it, until she could sort herself out and find something better. She had had hardly any clothes or personal effects as her trip to Paris was only supposed to have been for one day and all her luggage was still on Menorca. The Johnsons insisted on giving her an advance of wages so that she could buy herself what she needed, and Stacy had had no choice but to accept.

Since then she had been working daily in the café, ignoring the remarks of the workmen and un-employed youngsters who frequented the café most. In the last few days she had begun to feel very tired all the time and hardly able to stand on her feet. She had a slight cough and a sore throat, but in her present state she was almost unaware of these things. She had schooled her mind to feel nothing—it was easier than having to remember. She yawned, then coughed and rested herself against the glass cabinet which housed sandwiches and rolls.

There were not many people in this evening, and she was glad. It was an effort to concentrate on anything and she vaguely wondered if there was something seriously wrong with her.

Mr Johnson looked across at her. 'Are you all right, lass? You look proper peaky to me. If I were you I'd go and have a rest. It's nearly closing time anyway, we can manage.'

'Oh, thank you, I am feeling a bit rough,' Stacy told him. 'I'll make the time up tomorrow.'

Mr Johnson flapped his hands, dismissing her words. 'Get way with you, half an hour or so makes no odds. Would you like Mrs J. to make you some tea?'

'No, no, it's quite all right, I think I'll go to bed early and get a good night's sleep.'

She went wearily up the stairs to her little bedsitter above the café. Her chest felt tight and she felt very dizzy. In the kitchenette she put the kettle on and reached for her hot water bottle to soothe her aching back. After making coffee and filling the bottle she went to bed, relieved to be off her feet at last. She awoke in the night with a searing pain in her head. It was difficult to open her eyes and she now ached all over. As her consciousness returned she realised that the awful rasping sound she could hear was coming from her own lungs.

Trying to sit up was difficult, every move she made was an effort and her breathing got worse with every attempt. She flopped back on to the pillows, gasping for breath and very frightened. The effort made her cough desperately and it became almost impossible to get her breath. Fortunately, Mrs Johnson must have heard her coughing, because some minutes later there was a knock on the door.

'Stacy love, are you all right?'

Stacy could only manage a stifled croak, but Mrs Johnson heard it. She came hurrying in.

'Oh, my, my, I think we'd better call in the doctor,' she said, after looking at Stacy. She shouted for her husband to ring while she tried to calm her down.

'There, there, lovey, you'll be all right now, the doctor will be here in a minute.'

To Stacy it seemed like hours before he arrived. She clung to Mrs Johnson's hand like a lifeline and refused to let go. The doctor diagnosed pneumonia and Stacy was taken immediately to hospital.

'My, you're looking better today,' Mrs Johnson said, a week later. 'Too thin, of course, but definitely more colour in your cheeks. They'll be letting you out soon, I suppose. Never keep anyone long in hospital these days.' She fished in her shopping bag and brought out two paperbacks. 'Mr Johnson sent these for you to read if you feel up to it.' She held them out and Stacy took them gratefully.

'Thank you, you've been very kind,' she said sincerely. 'I'm sorry to have caused you so much trouble.'

'No trouble, my dear. We're only happy to help. I hope someone would do the same for my daughter if she was taken bad away from home. Mr Johnson sends his regards. I'll come again tomorrow,' said

Mrs Johnson, standing up and kissing Stacy on the cheek before she left the room.

As Stacy watched her go, she knew she could not go back to work at the café. She was not cut out for that type of work and felt she must make a new life for herself. She had qualifications, she should surely be able to find a more suitable job.

The nurse came in a little later, smiling broadly. 'Well, how are you feeling now, Stacy? You look much better,' she said.

'Oh, fine. When can I leave?'

The nurse laughed. 'Oh, surely we're not that bad, are we? I'm afraid it's up to doctor, he'll let you know. Anyway, I have some good news for you—you have a visitor. Come in, Señor Cuevas, Stacy can see you now.'

'No!' Stacy shouted. 'I won't see *him*—send him away, please!'

The nurse looked startled. 'But, Stacy, he says he's your fiancé—surely you want to see him?'

'No, I don't—please get rid of him,' Stacy begged, but stopped short when Felipe walked through the door.

'Hello, Stacy,' he said. His voice sounded very tired and he had obviously lost some weight.

'I don't want to speak to you—go away!'

'Stacy, for God's sake, I have been chasing you half way across the world . . . I tried every hospital in London, on the offchance that you might have had an accident . . .'

'I don't care about that, you shouldn't have bothered. Go away!'

'No, I must speak to you—I don't understand what has happened. You have to tell me.'

'I don't owe you any explanations, Señor

Cuevas—if you don't know then I don't intend to explain it to you.'

'You must give me an explanation—what have I done to deserve this treatment?'

'Go away!' Stacy shouted at the top of her voice. 'Just go away or I'll scream!'

The nurse came to her side and tried to calm her.

'I'm afraid you'll have to leave, sir, I can't risk my patient getting hysterical, she's been very ill, you know.'

Felipe turned his troubled eyes to Stacy, but she refused to look at him. She sobbed bitterly into the ample bosom of the nurse and did not even hear Felipe turn dejectedly away and leave the room. When she realised he had gone she pushed herself upright.

'I want to see the doctor—how do I discharge myself from here?'

'But you can't do that, you're not well enough to leave here yet!'

'I'm sorry, but I must. If you won't fetch the doctor or whoever has to O.K. it I'll just get up and walk out now.'

'No, you mustn't do that. Stay here and I'll fetch Sister,' the nurse said.

By the time she returned with the Sister Stacy had cleared her locker and packed her things into a polythene bag. She was dressed and sitting wearily on the side of the bed, exhausted by her efforts.

'Now, now,' the Sister said, bustling around Stacy and trying to get her to lie on the bed. 'What's all this about?'

'I'm discharging myself,' Stacy told her firmly. 'I'm very grateful for what you've done, but I must leave now. What do I do? I have to sign something, don't I?'

Mrs Johnson was astounded to see her on the doorstep.

'Good gracious, child, what are you doing here?' she exclaimed, stepping aside to let Stacy in.

She walked past Mrs Johnson and into the living room. 'Sit down,' Mrs Johnson told her. 'Why on earth didn't you phone and let us know they'd let you come home?'

'I discharged myself,' Stacy admitted. 'I have to get away, Mrs Johnson. Someone came to see me today whom I didn't want to see at all. I shall go mad if I don't get away—I can't face seeing him again. I've come to collect my things.'

Mrs Johnson stared, her face almost comical in her surprise.

'Where will you go?' she asked.

Stacy shook her head. 'I don't know, to be honest, I don't know at all.'

She put her head in her hands and cried pitifully. Mrs Johnson put her arms around the distraught girl and rocked her backwards and forwards.

'Now, now, don't get so upset. There's always a solution to a problem. How would you like to go and stay in our bungalow in Dorset for a bit? There's no one using it at the moment, you'd be welcome to go there.'

Stacy looked up through tear-soaked lashes. 'Oh, Mrs Johnson, you're an angel! I'd be very grateful to you if I could go there for a while.'

'Well, that's settled, then. When would you like to go?'

'Oh, as soon as possible, please—now.'

'Oh dear, you are in a hurry, aren't you? Surely it can't be as bad as all that?'

'Oh yes, it can,' Stacy assured her. 'Maybe I'm being silly, but—well, I can't help it. I have to get away and that's that.'

'Well, there's no problem there, dear. Don't go upsetting yourself any more. You can go to the bungalow whenever you want. But you need a good night's rest first—you look as if you're going to pass out.'

'But . . .' Stacy began.

'No buts,' Mrs Johnson insisted. 'You stay in bed for the rest of the day and try to relax. I'll arrange your train ticket and everything else that's necessary. Now, just do as I say. Nothing's going to happen between now and then. You can go by the first train in the morning.'

'Oh, thank you, thank you so much. I'll pay you back one day for all your kindness, I really will.'

'I told you before, it's only what I hope someone would do for my daughter if she needed help.' She looked at Stacy, a worried expression on her face. 'Are you sure you don't want to talk about it?' she asked.

Stacy shook her head. 'No, I'm sorry, I really don't feel up to it at the moment. But thank you for trying to help.'

'Well then, off you go upstairs, I'll bring you a hot drink in a minute.'

'Oh, I couldn't face one . . .'

'You'll just have to try, my girl. If you won't do as I say I shall fetch the doctor to you. How can you go and stay by yourself in that condition? You've got to use your common sense or you'll have no choice but to end up in hospital again.'

Stacy couldn't argue with her logic and went

meekly up the stairs to her old room. By the time
she had undressed and crawled wearily between the
sheets Mrs Johnson arrived with her drink. Stacy
drank it without protest and Mrs Johnson was well
pleased. She tucked her up and told her to try to
sleep while she made the arrangements for the journey. After the shock of seeing Felipe again, the diffi-
culty of discharging herself from hospital and the
long, arduous journey across London she found it
difficult to sleep. Thoughts of all the good times she
had shared with Felipe flashed through her mind—
the night in Paris which should have been so happy
and had turned out so sour; all the things which
Chris had told her. Eventually her tired body relaxed
into an uneasy sleep.

She woke up once during the evening when Mrs
Johnson came in with a light meal which she ate
obediently. It was early when she awoke the following morning, the alarm clock said six. Mrs Johnson
could be heard moving around in the kitchen downstairs and Stacy got up slowly and took a quick bath.
As she was packing away her last bits and pieces a
knock came at her door.

'Are you awake, Stacy love?'

'Yes, Mrs Johnson—come in,' she replied.

'Ah, you're up already! You're eager to get away
from us, aren't you?'

'Oh no, not from you,' Stacy said sincerely.

'Well, that long sleep has done you good, you've
got a bit more colour in your cheeks this morning,
but you're far too thin. You'll have to make sure
you eat properly—you will do that, won't you?'

'Yes, Mrs Johnson, I promise.'

'And try to cheer up a bit. I know you think it's
the end of the world at the moment, but I'm sure

everything will turn out right in the end. Oh, I know that sounds corny and all that, but you mark my words, I'll be proved right yet.'

Stacy managed a weak smile. 'I hope so,' she replied, wondering how things could ever be right again.

Mrs Johnson had prepared her a good breakfast. Stacy was forced to eat it for fear of not being allowed to leave, although it was an extreme effort. The train left at eight-fifteen and Mr Johnson drove her to the station and carried her bags to her compartment. She waved a tearful goodbye to the couple and settled back in her seat, hoping the journey wouldn't take too long. She was glad to have the compartment to herself and slept for most of the way.

The Johnsons had arranged for a taxi to pick her up at the station, for which Stacy was grateful, as she was feeling very ill by the time she arrived. The driver took her to the door and carried her small case for her. The bungalow was pretty. There were climbing roses around the door and a neat, well thought out garden.

'There you are, miss—are you quite certain you're all right? You don't look very well to me.'

'Yes,' Stacy assured him firmly, 'I'm fine, thank you.' She handed him a tip and turned to open the door.

It was marvellous to sink down on to the soft sofa and rest her aching head and limbs. It was there some five hours later that Felipe found her, tossing and turning in a fevered sleep. Stacy was quite oblivious of him carrying her into the bedroom and undressing her overheated body, of him carefully wiping her face and neck with a cool flannel, and of him sitting with her almost constantly for the next three days and nights.

Felipe had called in a doctor immediately and he came in each day to monitor her progress. Felipe had asked if it was absolutely necessary for her to go into hospital and the doctor had had to agree that it was not—as long as she had someone to look after her at all times the fever would eventually abate with the aid of the antibiotics he had prescribed. Felipe knew that she would take the first opportunity to discharge herself again if she realised that he had caught up with her and he didn't want to take the chance of losing her again, so he sat with her day and night, listening to her unintelligible ramblings and waiting for her to recover.

On the fourth day Stacy woke up for a short while. She looked blankly at Felipe as he leaned over her, but showed no sign of recognition. He managed to get her to swallow some clear soup a little later, but she still did not know him. When she was sleeping again he went into the kitchen and made himself a cup of black coffee. He sat down in the lounge for a moment on the comfortable sofa and rested his head on the back. He had not realised just how much he would go through for the girl he loved. If someone had asked him a few months earlier whether he would chase half way across the world for a woman who had walked out on him and made him look a fool he would have been quite adamant that he would not. But he could not let Stacy go without finding out the reason for her change of heart. It was eating away at him day and night, he had to face her and find out exactly what had gone wrong.

His eyes felt heavy and, try as he might, he could

not resist sleep any longer. The long nights of sitting in a hard chair at Stacy's bedside had taken their toll and his head fell to one side and he slept.

By six o'clock the following morning Stacy was wide awake and feeling much better. She looked around the bedroom, wondering how on earth she had got there. The last thing she remembered was sitting down on the sofa in the lounge four days earlier. The chair close to her side surprised her too. It seemed as if someone else had been sitting in it, watching her. She felt weak, but could think quite clearly now and she stumbled to the bathroom, feeling in need of a wash.

The noise of her ablutions woke Felipe from his position on the sofa. He rubbed his neck and blinked; yes, there was definitely a noise coming from the bathroom. Stacy opened the door and he quickly walked out into the hall, startling her by his sudden appearance. He was amazed by the change in her. She was so thin, so pale, but he still found it difficult not to take her in his arms. Stacy almost fell when she realised who it was. At first she had thought he was an intruder; the dark beard, tousled hair and crumpled clothes did not look at all like the Felipe she remembered.

'You!' she spat out, holding on to the wall to steady herself.

'Yes, me,' he replied wearily. 'At last I have caught up with you.'

'Well, you can just get out!' Stacy shouted angrily, her head beginning to swim again. 'I have absolutely nothing to say to you—and you're trespassing. I'll call the police!'

'You have nothing to say to me?' he said bitterly. 'You walk out on me a couple of days before our wedding with no explanation—no apparent reason, but you say you have nothing to explain to me? Are you so hard-hearted that you think I do not even deserve that? I do not even know what I am supposed to have done.'

Stacy could feel her pale cheeks burning.

'You lied to me,' she countered.

'When?' he replied.

She faltered. She could not think of one occasion when he had actually lied.

'You didn't tell me the truth, anyway,' she defended herself.

'O.K., when did I not tell you the truth? When did I commit this deceit which caused you to desert me at the last minute?'

'You've been engaged before.'

'Yes, that is correct. It was many years ago. What possible difference does that make? Surely you are not jealous of that? If you knew that why did you not ask me about it yourself instead of running away?'

'You didn't tell me about her, and you should have done,' Stacy continued. 'You didn't tell me that she was English or that your family dislike English girls because of it. Your mother would never have accepted me into the family—that's why you didn't want me to meet them, not until we were married and it was too late.'

'That is nonsense, I do not know what you are talking about. Of course my family was bitter. If your family found that you had been deserted by your fiancé they too would be bitter. It is a natural reaction of the people who love you to suffer when you are upset. What possible difference would that make to our relationship?'

'Your mother would hate me because I'm English too.'

'Nonsense. She is not so stupid as to imagine that all English girls are tarred with the same brush— although now I am beginning to wonder.'

'Chris told me all about you,' Stacy told him, watching to see if he showed any reaction.

He raised his eyebrows. 'Oh yes? And what does your sister know about me that could poison your mind?'

Stacy swayed unsteadily and Felipe immediately scooped her up in his arms like a doll, carrying her effortlessly into the lounge and pinning her down on the sofa with his hands.

'*Dios*, you hardly weigh anything, what the hell have you done to yourself?' he muttered.

'Let go of me—I don't want you to touch me!'

'That,' he said icily, 'is quite obvious. But you must be a fool if you expected me to just shrug my shoulders at your disappearance. I do not give up so easily—and I want an explanation.'

'I've told you,' Stacy shouted at him, 'Chris told me all about you.'

'Told you what?' he shouted back.

'About you and her, for a start.'

'About *what*? There has never been anything between your sister and myself for her to tell you about.'

'Why should she lie?'

'How should I know?'

'She's my sister, there's no possible reason for her to say things that weren't true.'

'You are very naïve, Stacy. You think that just because she is your sister she cannot put a foot wrong—is that it?'

'I—I don't know. But as I say, what reason could she have for lying to me?'

Felipe rubbed his eyes with one hand, keeping Stacy in position still with the other. 'I do not know—what makes a woman's mind work anyway? *Dios*, I doubt that I shall ever know.'

Doubts had begun to creep into the corners of Stacy's mind. Felipe looked as bad as she felt and totally out of his normal respectability. With his unshaven face and unruly hair he looked like a pirate, ruthless and determined—but, she realised, she still loved him, even as she hated him.

'She told me you wouldn't leave her alone—that she had to threaten to tell Fernando before you'd stop,' Stacy told him moodily.

He was quiet for a few seconds, the only sound in the room was the ticking of the mantel clock.

'That is not true,' he said eventually. 'I will tell you the truth, and you can please yourself whether or not you believe me. Chris invited me over to dinner one evening while Fernando was away on business, and I accepted. I had dinner with them quite frequently and did not see any cause to refuse. I thought that perhaps Chris wanted someone to talk to in Fernando's absence. Everything was fine. The meal was good, the wine was excellent—it was a bottle produced from my own vineyards—but unfortunately Chris drank a little too much. She made some suggestions which I had to refuse and she wasn't very pleased. I managed to reason with her, or so I thought. I told her that it had been the wine talking and she should not worry about it. I thought it had all been forgotten a long time ago. I have made a point of never being alone with her again, but I did not let it interfere with my friendship with

Fernando. There has never been another occasion to which she could refer.'

Stacy listened numbly. He sounded convincing—but then so had Chris. 'Why should I believe your story instead of hers?' she asked.

Felipe shrugged. 'That is entirely up to you, Stacy. But let me tell you this. Fernando has been a friend of mine for a long time. I went to his wedding and congratulated him on his choice of bride—*his* choice, not mine. I do not deny that Chris is attractive, but I would no more make a pass at her than I would my own sister. I do not need to poach other men's wives. I have never had any trouble finding my own women—I do not need to borrow those of my friends.'

Stacy felt near to tears again. She was torn between loyalty to her sister and love for Felipe, and her confused mind could not distinguish which one to believe.

'I still don't understand all this,' she muttered.

'Chris is either jealous or frightened that I might mention her outburst at the dinner party to you. I would never have done so if you had not forced my hand.'

Tears streamed down Stacy's cheeks now. She felt weak and totally confused.

'I mean to know exactly what happened in Paris,' Felipe told her. 'Your tears will not make me change my mind.'

Stacy couldn't reply. The tears continued to flow and she did nothing to stop them.

'My patience is wearing thin. I am tired and I am angry. I have chased you half way across the world and I do not intend to give up now.'

'Oh God, I feel sick,' Stacy spluttered.

'Not half as sick as I felt when I found out what you had done, I assure you,' Felipe replied. 'I do not like being made a fool of.'

'*I* make a fool of *you*?' she repeated. 'I thought it was the other way around! It was me who was hoodwinked. I can't think what pleasure you would have got from ruining my life.'

'Ruin . . .? Why should I do that? I thought I was going to make you happy.'

'How could you do that? Did you think I wouldn't find out about Chris? She told me everything, but like a fool I ignored her. I fell for your phoney kisses and sweet words—just as you intended. Does it make you happy to know that you've made my life a misery? Are you happy now, Felipe?'

He stood up and looked down at her, his face a cold mask, his eyes roving her face as if trying to make sense of her words.

'Do I look happy?' he asked.

Stacy turned her head away. 'You're not making sense—why should I want to make you unhappy?'

'Well, if you don't know by now, it's a waste of time me telling you.' He came down on his haunches beside her, shaking her shoulders roughly. 'You will tell me what she has been saying. If I have to sit here all day you will tell me!'

Stacy looked down into her lap. The feel of his hands burning through her thin housecoat made her mind whirl. She could not think straight when he was touching her.

'I told you—she said you'd tried to seduce her.'

'And you believed that of me? You really believed that I would seduce the wife of my best friend? Oh, Stacy, how could you? I thought you said you loved me.'

'She told me how you enjoy leading women on—English women—just to let them down at the last minute. She said it was because you'd been let down—to salve your bruised ego.'

Felipe shook his head in disbelief. 'She is a good actress, your sister. She smiles sweetly to my face and twists a knife into my back from behind. Come back to Menorca and marry me.'

'No!' Stacy shook her head violently. 'I couldn't—it's just no good, Felipe.'

He looked up at her, his face hard and implacable. 'I see, so it was all a put-on from the start—a plot hatched between you and your sister to amuse yourselves. She must really hate me—but you—you are the best actress of them all. I really believed you cared for me. You certainly had me fooled.'

'No!' she shrieked. 'Why try to put the blame on me? You started this fiasco!'

She burst into floods of tears again, sobbing uncontrollably. The fact that Felipe just stood and watched made it much worse. He made no move to help or comfort her, and her misery grew by the second. She tried to find a handkerchief but didn't seem to have one. Suddenly a clean white square was thrust into her hand.

'Use this,' was all he said.

Stacy rubbed viciously, but the tears would not stop. It was the first time she had really let herself go since returning to England and all her pent-up emotions seemed to give way at once. She stood up and rushed past Felipe, heading for the bedroom and sanctuary. But she didn't even make it through the door before he grabbed her arm and swung her around to face him. His eyes softened momentarily as he surveyed her devastated face, but the expression was almost immediately replaced by the impersonal mask he had worn before, his voice was husky but cold.

'So—still you try to run. Your running days are over, Stacy—they cannot go on for ever, and I do not intend to pursue you any further.'

'Felipe,' she begged, 'let me sit down, please. I don't feel very well.'

He studied her face. 'Very well, you have been extremely ill. You were a fool to discharge yourself from hospital as you did.'

'I didn't want to see you,' she replied.

'And you endangered your life to get away from me. Do you realise that if I had not found you here you might have died?'

Stacy looked startled. 'What happened? I can't remember.'

'You were lying on the sofa when I arrived—in a high fever. You needed antibiotics immediately to clear the infection in your lungs.'

He was very close to her on the sofa. Her perverse brain longed for him to put his arms around her and comfort her. She wanted to feel his heart beating close against her own and his laboured breathing as he tried to control his emotions, like it had been before.

'I told you I would never do anything to hurt you, that I loved you to distraction. Why did you not believe me?' he muttered, more to himself than to her.

She looked into his face, her eyes searching for just a flicker of compassion.

'Thank you for staying to help me,' she said eventually. 'You obviously saved my life.'

Felipe did not respond. He stared straight ahead, his face weary and strained.

'Felipe,' she said softly, her hand running down the side of his unshaven neck. She felt him stiffen and could not bear the thought of his rejection at that moment. She flung her arms around his neck, burying her face against his shoulder.

'Oh, Felipe,' she begged, 'please hold me.'

For a moment she thought he was going to push her away. His body was rigid, but inevitably he found himself winding his arms around her slight body. She lifted her head to look at his face and almost immediately his lips plundered hers in a kiss which was more punishment than pleasure. Stacy moaned as she tasted blood from the soft inner flesh of her lips, but Felipe did not release her. She found herself lying on the sofa with him above her. This time he was kissing her tenderly, arousing all the old feelings inside her which she could not prevent. No matter what he had done in the past, she loved him still.

He kissed her swollen eyelids and her ears, then ran his tongue softly down the side of her neck.

'Stacy,' he breathed hoarsely, 'I can tell that you still want me—why did you do it? Why did you run away without asking me for an explanation?'

She did not answer. She wanted him to continue making her feel alive again. She pulled his head back down to her own and kissed him.

Taken unawares, Felipe could do nothing to stop her. The weight of his body and the sensuous stroking of his hands was all she could think of—nothing else mattered at that moment. Chris and her accusations were forgotten.

CHAPTER SEVEN

SUDDENLY she was lying alone. Felipe pushed himself away from her and stood up, his back towards her. He ran a long brown finger around the back of his neck and then turned back to her.

'This is no good, Stacy. We have to talk. Please get up,' he said stiltedly. 'I will go and make some coffee. You must wash your face in cold water, it will reduce the swelling of your eyelids.'

Stacy felt awful; she had forgotten that she must look a sight. Immediately she left the room and went to the bathroom to tidy up. The face looking back at her in the mirror was ravaged. Only her eyes, under the puffy lids, looked bright—the memory of Felipe's lovemaking bringing a sparkle to them. She rested her head on the cool tiles at the side of the washbasin and took a deep breath. Everything seemed so stupid now. She realised that she should have confronted Felipe with Chris's accusations and given him the chance to defend himself. Now he was with her she had grave doubts about her sister's truthfulness. As Felipe had said, he did not look like a man who was enjoying himself.

When she returned to the sitting room he had made the coffee and was sitting on the sofa drinking a cup. He motioned her to join him and she did so.

'Stacy,' he said softly, 'you must tell me everything that happened in Paris. I have to know. I cannot fight what I do not understand.'

She took a large sip of coffee and held the cup in both hands to warm them. 'Chris had been making remarks from the beginning,' she began. 'She told me not to get involved with you—but I couldn't help myself. She said you wanted to marry me because you couldn't have her—I've never seen her as she was in Paris. She'd had too much wine and I was so happy, I suppose I was going on a bit—but she started on me viciously, saying terrible things about you. It was such a shock I didn't know what to believe. She said you'd repeatedly made passes at her and she threatened to tell Fernando and then you stopped.'

'Bitch,' Felipe said abruptly.

'What's it all about, Felipe? Tell me!'

'I do not know. From what you have said I assume she is jealous of your relationship with me. I think she thought she had got above her family beginnings—that she had bettered herself. I suppose when she saw that you were climbing even higher up the social ladder she felt cheated out of her glory. It is only a guess,' he added, shrugging.

'You could be right,' Stacy pondered. 'I remember her telling me I'd be better off with some down-to-earth English boy.'

'She had no right to try and ruin your life.'

'Tell me about the other girl, Felipe, the one you were engaged to,' Stacy begged him, needing to know, but not really wanting to hear.

He sighed and put his cup on the floor. 'I *was* engaged to an English girl once. It was many years ago and I was young and foolish. I did not realise what I was doing—she would never have suited me anyway. I was heartbroken at the time; I suppose I felt angry at being let down. Of course my parents were angry about it—as any parents would be. But it is all in the past. It did not make me bitter towards English girls—you should have known that by my reactions to you. If you had been more experienced you would have known what you were doing to me. I was dubious of forming a permanent relationship with anyone until I met you. But with you I was sure,' he said, taking her pale face between his hands and kissing the tip of her nose affectionately. 'I know I shall never need anyone but you—that is what made me follow you.'

'Oh, Felipe, I'm such a fool! I've made myself ill and you unhappy—I even thought of committing suicide at one time. Will you forgive me?'

He moved even closer and kissed her neck tantalizingly. 'I'm sure you can make me forget the torment you have put me through. I shall make you pay me back in full for all of it, every bit.'

'Good,' Stacy replied, 'I shall look forward to it.'

'Wanton,' he chided. He kissed her thoroughly, and then his eyes hardened. 'I hope Chris feels suitably chastised over this affair. You gave her a nasty shock when you ran away. I think she thought we would guess that it was her fault and tell Fernando. She was quite genuinely upset by your disappearance.'

'I don't think I can ever forgive her,' Stacy replied.

'You must try. Jealousy is a terrible affliction—I know, I suffer it constantly because of you. I do not think she was capable of stopping herself, she was far too caught up in her own feelings to think of yours.'

'You won't tell Fernando, will you, Felipe?' she begged. 'I think he would be very angry if he knew.'

'I would not dream of it. Fernando is my friend. I would do nothing to hurt his feelings if I could avoid it. Anyway, I think Chris will have learned her lesson.'

'I hope so,' Stacy replied.

'Now,' said Felipe, 'tell me what happened to you. How did you get back to England, and why were you so ill?'

'I caught the ferry from Boulogne, but to be quite honest, I don't really remember much about it. I was in such a state I acted like a zombie. I eventually found my way to London and went to the Johnsons' café for a cup of coffee. I was worn out and I suddenly found myself crying. I couldn't stop, and the Johnsons were very kind to me. They listened to my story and offered me the use of their bedsitter above the café. They gave me a job as well. At the time I just didn't care and I accepted. It was hard being on my feet all day and I wasn't really bothering about myself. I didn't eat regularly and I suppose I was just weak and caught pneumonia because of that.'

'And you discharged yourself from hospital like an idiot before you were better.'

'I couldn't face you, Felipe. I was so confused, so unhappy. I just felt as if I needed to be on my own.'

'I suffered agony when I found out what you had done,' he told her. 'I came back to the hospital in the evening and you had disappeared. The hospital gave me the Johnsons' address, but by the time I arrived there the following morning you had gone again. I was frantic with worry—I had visions of you flaking out on the train with no one to look after you.'

'I didn't feel very well, I must admit. All I can remember is sitting down on the sofa here to rest my legs. I'm so sorry, Felipe, I really am. I should have had more sense than to think I could escape you so easily. I should have stayed and faced you.'

'Indeed you should. But I think we should forget the past and start again. You do want to start again, don't you?'

'Oh yes, yes! I love you, I never really wanted to run away, I just couldn't cope with what Chris had said.' She closed her eyes and held her throbbing head. 'Oh, I do feel rough,' she moaned.

Felipe stood up immediately. 'But of course—I am a fool. You must go back to bed immediately. I will make you some breakfast—look, it is nearly eight o'clock. You have not eaten for days, you must be starving.'

'I suppose I am quite hungry,' Stacy agreed. 'But I don't feel up to much, and I'm sure I can get it myself.'

'You will go back to bed immediately. I will bring you some scrambled eggs—I can manage those quite well—and some thin slices of toast.'

'Sounds delicious,' she replied.

She walked towards the bedroom. 'Felipe,' she said, turning around at the door, 'what will you do, while I'm in bed?'

'Well,' Felipe said with a slight smile, 'I shan't be joining you, that is for sure. You are not well and I am so tired that I think I shall sleep for the rest of the day also. But tomorrow . . . who knows what will happen? You need some food inside you and a good rest—I want you back in perfect health.'

Stacy smiled radiantly for the first time in weeks and went happily back to bed. Felipe did not take long to bring her breakfast and he sat with her until she drifted into sleep again. He crept out of her bedroom and went to lie in the comfortable guest bedroom next to Stacy's and slept untroubled for the first time in what seemed like years.

When Stacy woke she could hear him talking and she stumbled out of bed to see who it was. As she reached her bedroom door he put the receiver down and turned to her.

'How do you feel?' he asked. Stacy was surprised by the change in him. He had shaved and changed into a pair of well worn jeans and a tee-shirt, and she longed to run into his arms again.

'I feel much better—it must have been your scrambled eggs that did it.'

He put his arm around her and led her into the lounge.

'Who were you speaking to on the phone?' she asked.

'Your father. I had to let him know I had found you safe.'

'Oh, poor Dad, I'd forgotten about that,' she said sheepishly.

Felipe seated her on the sofa and sat down beside her. 'He sends you his love,' he told her, 'and wants to see you as soon as possible. I told him we would go home at the end of the week.'

'What are we going to do till then?' she asked.

'We will have to see,' he replied noncommittally. 'We must send for the doctor to give you a thorough check-up.'

'But I feel much better,' Stacy argued.

'It is of no matter, you must still see the doctor. I will ask him to call later this morning.'

'Morning?' Stacy queried. 'Surely I haven't slept all through yesterday and last night?'

'Oh yes, you have, my darling. I looked in on you many times and you did not stir. Although I must admit I slept a lot myself.'

'Oh, Felipe, I'm so happy! I didn't think I'd get a second chance. I thought you would hate me.'

'I did hate you, believe me. I could have killed you when I first found out what you had done. It is a good job you had left the country—if I had caught up with you in those first days there is no telling what I might have done.'

'Could you really murder me?' she asked, her eyes wide and appealing.

He swiftly kissed her upturned lips. 'I do not suppose I could, although it would have been uppermost in my mind. It is hard for me to explain. I do not like feeling vulnerable, it is a new experience for me; you make me feel vulnerable, Stacy. It was the first time in my life that a woman had power over me. When you walked out of my life I felt as though a limb was missing. But no, I could not have killed you; once I had you in my arms—well, I'm sure the outcome would have been more pleasant. I am in a bad way, Stacy, and it is all your fault.'

'Mmm, I'll have to try and help you get better,

then,' she said, smiling at him cheekily.

Felipe could not resist the temptation and pulled her into his arms, there beside the telephone in the hall, and kissed her until she could hardly breathe. When he released her he was breathing raggedly and so was Stacy.

'Does this house have a drinks cabinet?' he asked. 'I think I could do with some rum in my coffee—if they have any. For medicinal purposes, of course,' he concluded.

'Yes, I think there should be some rum. Mr Johnson was in the Navy.'

They hunted through the lounge and found some bottles in the sideboard. Felipe insisted that he would make them some breakfast and Stacy returned to her bedroom to sort out some clothes before having a shower. By the time she had washed and dressed he had finished cooking their breakfast and she went towards the delicious smell coming from the kitchen.

'It smells gorgeous,' she said, standing in the doorway.

Felipe looked up and surveyed the tiny figure. Her dress was far too big now and hung off her in all the wrong places, but he still felt the same stirring inside him as he had before.

'Come and sit down and eat this, we must fatten you up before your father sees you.'

He had prepared bacon, egg, tomatoes and fried bread, and Stacy was quite surprised at his expertise in the kitchen.

'I didn't know you could cook,' she said, tucking into her first real meal for some time.

'I am quite domesticated—just because someone else usually does it for me it does not mean that I have not attempted it myself. Unless there are many people on board I always do the cooking on the yacht. I prefer it that way.'

'A man of many talents,' Stacy quipped.

'When are we going home?' she asked some time later when they were drinking their coffee laced with rum.

'Home?' Felipe replied.

'Yes, back to Menorca. I want to go back there with you. I was so happy there when you were with me, except when Chris was putting doubts into my mind.'

'You have no more doubts, *amada*?'

She shook her head. 'No, I have no doubts, Felipe, none at all.'

'That is good. I have a special licence with me. I intend to marry you immediately, before you can escape me again.'

'Oh, Felipe,' Stacy screamed, running around the table and flinging herself at him, 'I can't believe it— I can't wait!'

Felipe fended her off for a moment. 'Do not distract me, *querida*, give me a chance to speak.'

'Yes?' she said impatiently.

'We will be married on Thursday—on Friday we will have the day together and on Saturday we are booked on a flight for Menorca. We will spend Friday in London, I think—to be near the airport.'

'You've been busy, haven't you?' Stacy teased.

'Yes, I don't intend anything to go wrong again.'

'Oh, Felipe, it won't, I know it won't. Mrs Johnson was right, she said everything would work out in the end. I like the Johnsons.'

'That is good, because I have invited them to be witnesses at our wedding—you do not mind?'

Stacy looked amazed. 'No, I don't mind at all,' she told him, 'in fact I'm delighted.'

'They were very good to you, I understand—not that they said so themselves, but I could tell that they thought a lot of you. I have also invited them to come to Andalusia in two months' time when we will have a formal ceremony at the chapel on the estate. We cannot waste that beautiful wedding dress you left behind—and my mother will be most upset if she is cheated out of the wedding celebrations.'

Stacy's eyes filled with tears. She hugged Felipe tightly, unable to speak for fear of crying.

'I love you,' she mumbled when she had control of herself.

'Keep telling me, *querida*,' he said softly against her ear. 'Because I love you too, and I want the feeling to be mutual.'

Three days later they were married. Mrs Johnson turned up in her best Sunday hat and dabbed a lacy handkerchief to her eyes when she saw Stacy. Mr Johnson looked smart in his best suit and they both wished the couple every happiness. Mrs Johnson still fussed over Stacy's slim figure, and after the ceremony Felipe took them for a meal at the Dorchester. Stacy would not have cared where they went, she only had eyes for Felipe, but Mr and Mrs Johnson were overwhelmed by the surroundings and the service they received, and couldn't wait to write to their relatives about it. They presented Stacy and Felipe with a beautiful crystal loving cup as a wedding present and they were pleased with the response it received. Stacy promised to put it in a prominent position in their home.

When the Johnsons left them Felipe took Stacy for a walk around Hyde Park before taking her back to their room at the Dorchester. He took her into his arms as he closed the door of their suite, and Stacy was swept away by the tide of his emotions and her own. He was kind and gentle with her and made her first experience of complete lovemaking a pleasurable one. She lay in his arms afterwards in the early evening gloom, smoothing her hand over his heated brow.

'Felipe, will it always be like this?' she asked childishly.

'Oh no, *querida*,' he told her, 'it will get better and better through all the years of our lives together. I intend to make sure of that.'

Two weeks later they lay on the beach on a tiny island off Greece. Felipe had been for a swim and was just walking up the beach and back to Stacy. She reached up a hand and fastened it around his ankle, running her fingers tantalisingly up his wet leg. He shivered and came down beside her immediately, removing the bra of her bikini and cupping her breasts with shaking hands.

'You do not need to wear this here,' he told her huskily. 'There is no one to see you but me.'

Stacy blushed. Even after two weeks together she was still shy of her own body. Felipe bent to kiss her exposed breasts and she squirmed beneath him.

'I cannot get enough of you,' he whispered into her neck. 'I did not believe anything could be so perfect.'

They had flown back to Menorca the previous week and Stacy had made a strained peace with her sister. Henry Barker had noticed nothing of the atmosphere, only glad that his daughter was back in their care and getting well again. He had been a little upset by their sudden marriage, but understood Felipe's concern to keep her near him. He was delighted when Felipe told him that they would go through another ceremony after their honeymoon, so that the family could take part in their happiness.

They had sailed on Felipe's yacht to the island of Koristos which belonged to a friend of his who loaned it to them for a month. It was uninhabited apart from the house of his friend and they had to get their supplies from a neighbouring island, but they did not mind. It meant total freedom to do as they pleased without fear of being watched. Stacy had been overawed by the beauty of the place. It abounded with flowers of every description and colour and was the proud possessor of an ancient temple.

'Are you happy, *querida*?' Felipe asked some time later.

Stacy took his face between her hands. 'How can you ask me that?' she smiled. 'Surely you must know how happy I am. I can't believe all this has happened to me.'

'You had better believe it,' he chided. 'You are Señora Felipe Cuevas now. I am sorry I dropped my title so many years ago, I would have liked to have given it to you.'

'I don't need to be a *condesa*,' Stacy replied. 'I'm quite happy to be Señora Cuevas.'

Felipe looked her over with affection. 'I am glad

you do not mind,' he said, running his hands down both sides of her body. 'You have put back the weight you lost in your illness. Mrs Johnson would approve.'

'She'll be able to see for herself when she comes over,' Stacy replied happily. 'I'm very frightened of meeting your mother,' she added.

'Why should you be? She wrote to us, did she not, saying how happy she was for us—and how disappointed at not being able to organise it all.'

'Mmm. Still, she can have that pleasure when we get back to your estate, can't she? I'm quite nervous of meeting all your workers too.'

Felipe rolled over and pinned her to the soft sand. 'They will love you, *querida*. They will marvel at your beautiful hair—the colour of pale gold—and they will envy my choice of wife. When we have children they will rejoice with us about that too. They are a very loyal workforce.'

Stacy softly kissed the edge of his mouth. 'I still can't believe you've chosen me, my life's been so ordinary compared with yours.'

'Perhaps that is why I love you so much,' Felipe replied. 'You make me feel ten feet tall—but still manage to keep my feet on the ground.' He stood up and pulled her to her feet. 'Shall we go back to the beach house?' he asked.

'What for?' Stacy asked, knowing quite well why.

He pressed her to him and nibbled her ear until she could stand it no longer. 'Come with me and you will find out,' he whispered.

'How can I resist?' she laughed.

'I should hope you would not want to,' Felipe

replied, picking her up easily in his arms and running back up the beach with her.

Harlequin® Plus

SPANISH WORDS AND PHRASES

From time to time, we receive letters from readers requesting that we print glossaries of foreign words and phrases contained in books with exotic locales. We hope you find useful this list of Spanish terms used in *To Be or Not to Be,* their meanings and how to pronounce them. (The syllables to be stressed are underscored.)

Spanish	Pronunciation	English Equivalent
amada	ah-<u>mah</u>-dah	my love
bien	<u>bee</u>-enn	well
buenos dias	bway-nohs <u>dee</u>-ahss	good day, good morning
cara	<u>kar</u>-ah	dear
Dios	<u>dee</u>-ohs	God
finca	<u>feeng</u>-kah	estate, ranch
gaviota	gah-vee-<u>oh</u>-tah	sea gull
gracias	<u>grah</u>-see-ass	thank you
hasta mañana	<u>ah</u>-stah man-<u>yah</u>-nah	till tomorrow, see you tomorrow
hermosa	er-<u>moh</u>-sah	beautiful
Inglesa	eeng-<u>glay</u>-sah	Englishwoman
jaleo	hah-<u>lay</u>-oh	an Andalusian dance
jardín	har-<u>deen</u>	garden
muy	mwee	very
ola	<u>oh</u>-lah	wave (as in ocean wave)
pequeña	pay-<u>kayn</u>-yah	little girl
querida	kay-<u>ree</u>-dah	dear, darling
sala	<u>sah</u>-lah	living room
te quiero	tay kee-<u>ay</u>-roh	I love you
tu eres Alemaña	too ay-rays ah-lay-<u>man</u>-yah	are you German?

Readers rave about
Harlequin romance fiction...

"I absolutely adore Harlequin romances!
They are fun and relaxing to read, and
each book provides a wonderful escape."
—N.E.,* Pacific Palisades, California

"Harlequin is the best in romantic reading."
—K.G., Philadelphia, Pennsylvania

"Harlequin romances give me a whole new
outlook on life."
—S.P., Mecosta, Michigan

"My praise for the warmth and adventure
your books bring into my life."
—D.F., Hicksville, New York

*Names available on request.